Baptism of
Blood and Fire

a novel by
DAMON J COURTNEY

Novels by Damon J Courtney

THE DRAGON BOND TRILOGY

Baptism of Blood and Fire
The Burden of Faith
The Fate of Champions

damon@damonjcourtney.com
www.DamonJCourtney.com

For Julie.
Who always believes in me.
Even when I don't.

BAPTISM OF BLOOD AND FIRE

PRELUDE

SHE COULD SMELL the stench of man from within the cave even before her head had entered. The chill wind howled around her, muddling the scent, but she detected it just the same. She flared her nostrils and blew a puff of frosted air before snaking her head in deeper.

The dragon moved slowly, trying to be silent, as she shifted her massive bulk inside the cave. With each step her clawed foot cracked the ice and crushed the snow beneath it, echoing off the walls and down into her lair. She drew herself up slightly as her wings passed the mouth, clipping the icicles that hung from the ceiling and sending them crackling and crashing down around her.

She would not sneak up on whoever this was.

She decided on a different tact. Drawing a lungful of the bitterly cold air, she let out a great roar that shook the mountain around her, breaking off more ice and snow. She blew as long and as hard as she could, and the sound echoed through the entire cavern. When she finished, she paused and waited for the intruder to come running toward the only exit and into her waiting maw.

Nothing moved.

She waited, ready to spring, but no one came. She grew impatient. Sucking in another breath, she charged down into her lair. A few short steps brought her into the main cavern, and she paused just long enough to look around and find the intruder. He was standing near her nest.

Near her eggs.

Without another thought, she blew the air from her lungs, blasting it out in a blizzard of frost and ice. It swirled toward him in a great cone. She meant to extinguish his life in one great breath.

He stood motionless, his arms crossed.

The blast flew straight for him, large enough to envelope him whole. But at the last instant, it parted to either side. The cone split and flowed around him like a river around a great boulder. She blew harder, pushing every ounce of air from her lungs, trying to push through the unseen barrier.

"Stop this," he said evenly.

The dragon stopped and pulled her head back in surprise. She drew a second, quick breath and gave him another blast. He shook his head silently as that one too went around and over him without ever nearing his body.

"You really are the stupidest of your kind."

She stopped again, and her eyes went wide.

"Oh, you understand? I wouldn't have thought you smart enough."

She narrowed her eyes and crouched low, a growl

escaping her lips. She watched him and waited for him to move or speak. She noticed, for the first time, that he was an elf and not a human as she had thought. He was small, even for a humanoid. He looked puny and insignificant standing there in front her.

But elves could be dangerous.

She continued watching him, trying to formulate a plan of attack. She had hunted magical prey before, but none who could so easily render her greatest weapon ineffective without even moving a finger. She was not defenseless though. The strength in her teeth and claws was beyond measure, but she did not dare charge. This elf was a tricky one. And he was in her home.

She cared nothing of the eggs in the nest behind him, they were worthless to her. But her treasure, a horde she had amassed over her lifetime, stood open in a smaller cavern deeper within her lair. That was something she would not give up without a fight. She stared long and hard before finally speaking.

"What do you want?" she said.

Her voice growled the words as much as spoke them, and she thought surely he would not understand her. The tongue of men was known to her, but she had never had much cause to use it. Unlike some of her race, she had avoided the world of men for most of her life. She had learned their tongue from other dragons but had rarely spoken it aloud.

She looked the elf up and down, trying to discern his motives.

"You can take the eggs," she managed to say at last.

The elf smiled and crossed his arms. He looked her up and down and shook his head.

"You would give up your children to be rid of me? Truly your kind is one to be despised. In truth I had thought you abandoned them already. I have known only a few of the dark dragons who stayed to raise their young."

She paused and searched her mind for the right words.

"You want my eggs for your mages. I will sell them."

He shook his head again and sighed.

"I cannot decide which is more despicable. The dragons of light give their children freely to mankind in some grand gesture of goodwill to us all, and here you are, offering to sell yours to me. At least you don't pretend to be doing something noble. But then, you've already been selling your eggs, haven't you?"

She didn't know what else to say.

"You can take the eggs."

"I don't want your eggs, lizard, I want your head."

Her pride had suffered enough. She roared and charged across the cave. She was halfway to him when he unfolded his arms and pointed a finger at her, speaking only a single word. She did not recognize the language he spoke, but it mattered little. It affected her whether she understood it or not.

A wave crashed over her, dazing her mind and body. The legs beneath her were stripped of their power to move, and her eyes could no longer focus. Her body fell powerless to the ground in a thunderous boom that shook the cave. Icicles fell away from the ceiling and crashed down around her, many shattering against her glistening, white scales.

She couldn't move.

She tried to stand. Tried to will herself up. It was no use. Her body would not respond. She could still see and hear everything around her, but she could not move to react. The elf clucked his tongue and turned his back to her. She watched helplessly as he stooped to pick up the three eggs in her nest and placed them one by one into a pack he pulled from his back.

His task finished, he stood and turned back to her.

"I will make your death quick," he said.

Her body tensed in anger and frustration, but the roar in her belly would not come. He spoke words she did not understand and moved his hands in ways she had never seen. She watched them dance in front of him and saw thin blue threads of light spring from his fingertips as the volume of his voice increased. The magic flowed between his palms and through his fingers as he weaved it into what, she could not imagine. The words sounded strange to her ears. Almost like a song.

When he finished, he cupped his hands together and then opened them to reveal a small, orange ball of fire no bigger than a gemstone. He stared at her, and she saw the fire dance in his eyes as he gave the ball a little toss. It flew harmlessly across the cavern to land in the snow in front of her eyes. She could see the movement of the flames as they flickered like tiny candlelight.

Then it exploded in a torrent of fire.

The flames rolled across her perfect, white scales in waves, blackening them all and burning some completely from her body. The heat was unbearable. It radiated through her scaly armor and fried the skin beneath it. She wanted to cry out, to scream in pain, but her voice would not answer the call of her mind. Her great roar escaped as a whimper that fell powerless from her unmoving lips.

Her life was slipping away.

She prayed that any moment, the pain would end. Her lungs ached from the fire, and she drew each burning breath expecting it to be the last. A part of her wanted vengeance, to destroy this man. But the bigger part now wished for sweet, merciful death. But the pain did not end. The flames burned out, leaving a huge cloud of steam filling the cave, and still she felt it. When at last she could open her eyes again, the steam cleared, and she found the elf standing in exactly the same spot. He folded his arms in front of him and smiled.

"You are a bit tougher than I would have thought. That blast should have killed a white as young as you."

She felt some of the magic in her bonds loosen. She tried to open her mouth to speak, but the smoke and fire that had filled her lungs had left her without a voice. Her lips parted, and she could feel and hear them crack as bits of her blackened flesh fell away, but she could not speak. She closed her eyes and focused on the feeling of the cold stone beneath her cheek.

Sweet death awaited.

She heard a shuffle and opened her eyes to see him

pulling his pack onto his back. He walked closer and stood in front of her, eyeing his handiwork. She heard him start moving and knew he was casting another spell. She couldn't see his hands, but she heard the same words. The same song. The song that would summon the fire again.

He finished and took a step back. Without a word, he dropped a little, swirling ball of fire at his feet and then turned and walked past her prone form. She heard his heels clicking on the stone and the snow crunch beneath his feet as the sound faded into the distance.

Her body began to respond.

Her legs started to twitch as the fog cleared from her mind. Every muscle cried out as her body moved against the magical bond that held her. When she could move at last, she found a new pain. The fire had destroyed her body, and she was now left with nothing but agony with every tiny movement. With the greatest of effort, she managed to raise her head a few inches from the floor.

Then the fireball exploded, and she was stilled forever.

***

Velanon felt a blast of hot air blow past him as he exited the cave but didn't look back to see the flames. The warmth from the cave faded quickly, and the cold wind of the great mountains around him blew across his body and bit into his skin. The spells he had warded himself with kept the mountain winds from freezing him to death where he stood, but he could still feel the cold.

He drew his cloak up tighter around him and walked to the lip of the ledge. The dragon's cave was high up in the top of the mountain where the air was coldest, and there was no path to it without a treacherous climb over rock and ice. Which meant no way down either.

Unless you were someone of Velanon's talents.

With a whispered word and a flick of his wrist, he stepped from the ledge and drifted like a feather down the sheer face of the mountain. The wind blew hard from the side, blowing him off his course a little, but he made no move to correct it.

Let them come to me.

Beneath his feet, a group of large men watched and waited. They stared up at him from below, their heavy white furs making them almost blend with surrounding snow. They shuffled along the mountain path, staying just below him.

He continued his leisurely descent without bothering to look at them. When his feet finally touched solid rock, the group of them surrounded him. He smiled coolly and shielded his eyes with his hand as he looked up to meet the eyes of the one who stepped forward.

"Do not crowd me, Dahr."

The largest of the barbarians looked down at him with a snarl but took a few steps back just the same. The others followed their leader and backed off as well.

Velanon stripped off his pack and set it on the ground in front of them. They all leaned forward to peer inside, but all that was visible was a magical blackness. From the black void within the pack he pulled the three white dragon eggs and set them on the ground.

"You remember our bargain," Velanon said. "These are

your eggs alone. You will not sell them to anyone else who comes looking for them. Other than that, you may do with them whatever you and your people do. Eat them, breed them, fight them, it makes no difference to me."

The big man nodded.

"Where are my diamonds?" he said at last.

The elf covered his eyes and looked up again, locking the big man in a stare.

"That was not part of our deal, Chief. If you want the dragon's horde, you'll have to climb the mountain and get it yourself."

"The dragon is dead?"

"Of course."

"If the dragon is already dead, why didn't you just take the diamonds and bring them to me?"

"The bargain was the location of the dragon's lair in exchange for her eggs. If you want anything else, you and your men will have to fetch it."

The giant man sighed loud enough for the elf to hear over the wind that battered against them. The chief looked up the mountain to the cave above and snarled again.

"I've already killed the worm," Velanon said. "All you need do is climb up there and eat it."

"We could have killed the dragon ourselves."

"Yes, but I've already cooked it for you."

The chief looked down again at the elf and smiled. As his smile grew wider he broke into a laugh. The men behind him quickly joined in, creating a loud chorus that echoed across the mountainside and dwarfed even the mountain winds.

Velanon gave no hint of a smile. He picked up the pack and pulled it across his back once more and then started off down the mountain path. They all continued laughing for another few moments before they noticed he was gone.

"Remember what I said, Dahr," Velanon called back over his shoulder. "If I hear of you selling dragon eggs, to anyone, I will come back and destroy you."

The barbarian chief narrowed his eyes at the elf's back, but he made no move toward him. He looked back up the mountain to the cave high above and then turned back to the elf, but he was already gone.

CHAPTER ONE

IMPRINTING

THE DRAGON'S HEAD snapped and hissed as it swayed back and forth in warning. It let out a tiny screech and flapped its wings hard, sending the last bits of its shell flying. It craned its neck up and screeched again, louder this time, and then snapped out at the girl in front of it.

This was the moment Elody had waited three years of her life for, but her feet would not move. Her body was tense, but she could not will it to act. She took a deep breath and tried to move closer, but nothing responded.

The dragon began flapping about. Its movements were uncoordinated and clumsy. It tripped over the bits of shell and stone on the floor and flapped its wings to keep from falling, but even that only made the move seem all the clumsier. It started scrambling around the cave floor with no clear path or purpose.

Elody's legs finally answered her mind's call, but they took her in the wrong direction. She danced back as the dragon flapped out of the little nest it was in and started stumbling around trying to reach her. She panicked and backed up some more.

Though its eyes were mostly closed, it still tracked her every step. She scooted to the side, but it followed her, screeching at her. She went back the other way, and it followed her again. They repeated this dance several more times before it started to tire. As Elody skipped back to the left again, the dragon stumbled over some piece of its shell and fell to the floor with a thud.

Elody sucked in her breath and almost lunged forward to help it, but she stopped when its head shot up. She froze in place again and stared. She glanced up at the silver dragon that watched over the scene, but the great mother made no move and gave no indication of her feelings.

Elody looked slowly back down to the little dragon and watched quietly. As its erratic movements ceased, its head started to dip low. It finally came to rest on the ground in front of her. She could hear its breath coming in short, quick bursts.

She felt ashamed for being afraid, but she didn't know what else to do. After a few seconds, the dragon closed its eyes and looked as though it might fall asleep. She might lose her chance if she didn't move.

"Go on!" her master shouted.

"I can't move, Master!"

The dragon's head shot up in an instant and started screeching. Its wings flapped, and it was up and stumbling again. She waited, completely still, for it to stop and settle down. When it did, she looked over her shoulder to her master waiting far behind her.

"Throw the hare!" he called out.

She turned back, slowly this time to avoid sudden movement, and faced the wyrmling. Taking a dead rabbit from the pouch at her side, she flipped it forward to land on the ground in front of the dragon. She glanced up again at the giant silver form towering over the scene with calm eyes and looked for some kind of approval. The mother just stared back calmly and made no move to interfere.

The baby lunged forward and snapped at the sound of the carcass hitting the ground, snatching it up in its jaws. Elody jumped back in surprise at how quick it was even at only minutes old. As the dragon started to devour the first meal of its life, Elody smiled a little to herself. Despite her fears, things were going just as she was taught.

Elody watched the wyrmling tear into the flesh and fur of the rabbit and heard the bones snapping as its jaws broke them with each bite. Now that the dragon was occupied she took a chance to look it over. Its scales were a dull gray, not the bright, metallic silver of its kind. They must get brighter as it gets older. Even at minutes old it was bigger than she had imagined. She looked again to its mother towering above her and marveled at how the little creature before her would one day be that big.

"Now cast your spell of calming," she heard her master call from behind her, breaking her trance.

She pulled her gaze away from the dragon and concentrated. She touched the amulet at her neck and felt the magic from it flow into her fingertips. When she pulled her hands away, she could feel the familiar tingle in them. She began moving them slowly through the air, her fingers twitching and dancing in tight, intricate patterns as she weaved the threads of magic.

She had to stretch her arms up several times so that the giant sleeves of her robes would fall back to her elbows. She was not accustomed to casting in them. The dragon was preoccupied with its meal and made no move to attack her again, but she kept her movements small and precise all the same.

She finished weaving the magic and turned her palms up and spread them in front of her in a soft gesture. She slowly opened her eyes and watched.

Nothing happened.

"Master?"

She had practiced the spell hundreds of times. She knew it by heart. She had even used it to calm a horse in the village when it became agitated after a run in with a snake.

"Master? Nothing happened! The magic didn't work!"

"It worked, my dear. Look, it's already beginning to calm."

She turned back to look at the dragon again and did notice a small change in its demeanor. It was nearly done with its meal, but its movements were slower. Calmer. Its neck had grown slack, no longer taut and ready to strike.

"Now, my dear. Step forward slowly and then stand still. It will come to you."

This is it.

Elody nodded her head, mostly to herself, and

shuffled forward a few tiny steps. The dragon raised its head carefully and watched her. She took a few more steps forward until she knew she was well within the reach of its bite. She stopped moving and stood very still.

"Hello, baby," she said. "Do you remember me? Do you recognize my voice? I'm the one who's been singing to you. Do you remember the song?"

She opened her mouth nervously and began singing softly to the baby the song she had sung to her egg nearly every night of the last two years. Its head lifted curiously. Her voice cracked several times as she tried to get through the song, and each time its head cocked to the side. Then its neck snaked forward suddenly, startling her, and she felt its nose within inches of her chest. She finished the song with a quiver in her voice.

Reach out and touch it.

Elody's hand shook as she brought it forward. This was the first time, possibly the last time, she would ever touch her dragon. If the dragon accepted her, she would spend the rest of her life with this creature. If it rejected her, the bond she had worked so hard to form would be broken. She would be left empty and without magic.

Please remember me.

The wyrmling inhaled and took in Elody's scent, smelling her fully for the first time. She closed her eyes and silently prayed that all the spells she had worked so hard to cast on the egg had worked. It sniffed at her for several agonizing seconds while she tried to remain perfectly still. Despite her best efforts, her body trembled uncontrollably. With a final sniff, the dragon lowered its head and laid down on the cave floor at her feet.

It had accepted her.

Elody beamed as she looked up to the dragon mother and locked eyes with the massive beast. She reached her hand and then paused. Should ask permission? The giant silver dragon's scaly lips curled up in a knowing smile and nodded.

"He is your dragon now, Elody," she heard her master say.

My dragon.

She smiled and looked down. Her body still trembling, she knelt and reached her hand out to touch the back of its head. She rested her palm there for a while, thinking how hard its skin was. Not at all like the skin of the babies she had cared for in the village. Something in her mind clicked from what her master had said.

"A boy?" she asked, turning to look over her shoulder. "He's a boy?"

"Yes, he is a boy," he said.

"How can you tell?"

"My dear, I have been training dragonmages for most of my life, and I have seen more imprintings than you will see summers. He is a boy."

She nodded absentmindedly and felt stupid for asking. So much she didn't know. As she turned back, never lifting her hand, she felt the dragon's head lift off the dirt floor of the cave and press hard against her palm. She rubbed the top of his head harder, and a low rumble escaped his newborn lips. The dragon let out a satisfied breath and then laid his head back down.

"You must complete the imprint, Elody," her master said. "Speak the words and cast your spell so that the permanent bond may be formed."

Keeping her hand steady on his head, she chanted the words she had practiced nearly every day for the last three years of her life. She spoke the words calmly and without hurrying. She touched her other hand to the amulet around her neck and felt the magic flow from her hand and down to her other hand resting on the dragon's head. As she finished speaking, she moved her hand under his chin and lifted his head to stare into the eyes of her new, lifelong companion.

"I had no idea how much it would affect me," she said. "It was just an egg I kept for two years. A round, hard thing that I talked to and sang to but never moved or made a sound. And now here is this creature, I... I love him already."

"Then the imprint has worked, and the bond has been formed. Your life and his are now intertwined for all your years."

She smiled down at the little dragon who was already falling fast asleep and blowing puffs of dirt into the air with every huff of its strong lungs.

She heard footsteps behind her as her master approached and put his hand on her shoulder. She looked up and smiled, but he was looking high above them to the dragon mother who presided over the whole encounter.

Her master's hand closed around her shoulder as he

motioned her to her feet. He nodded to her and gently pushed her forward toward the feet of the great wyrm. She towered over them, her chest and neck casting a long shadow over the cave.

The Silver Queen.

"Great and mighty Kiranoth'ul'Daltharr," she began with a practiced measure, speaking the words exactly as she had been taught. "I give you my lifelong thanks for the gift that you have given me this day. My life and my power are owed to you."

The dragon smiled down at her and waited for her to finish.

"From this day forward, this wyrmling is mine to care for, as I am his, but you are his birthmother. He is of your blood. Would you honor me by naming your child?"

"Among his own kind," she began, as she had no doubt done many times before, "he shall be Jalthrax'ul'Daltharr."

Elody took the name in for a second, rolling it around on her tongue and trying to speak it silently to herself. It was hard for her to pronounce. It was something she would have to get used to. She realized the older dragon was waiting for her to speak.

"Thank you, Silver Queen, for this gift," she said. "I am forever in your debt."

She bowed low as she heard her master shuffle up behind her.

"Come, my dear," he said. "Our work here is done, and we must let Jalthrax sleep. In seven days time he will be ready to travel. You will come every day with food and sit with him until he is ready."

Elody nodded and looked down at him sleeping. She knelt and ran her hand across his head one last time and felt a pang of regret at having to leave him. But this was the way it was done.

"Thank you, Silver Queen," her master said as he tugged on her shoulder.

She stood up tall and walked with her master out of the cave and into the bright sunlight. Her master put his hand on her shoulder and turned her gently to face him. She saw a big smile on his face that stretched from one ear to the next.

"You did brilliantly, my dear. Exactly as I taught you. The imprint could not have been more perfect."

"Thank you, Master. I could not have done it without you."

She saw her brother Rinn approaching out of the corner of her eye, and she glanced back to see the smile on her master's face quickly fade.

"Did it work?" Rinn asked.

Elody smiled and bobbed her head. Rinn smiled back at her, but she saw him turn away as her master stepped toward her. He took her hand and walked with her to the bottom of the mountain. They chatted with a carefree air the whole way down, the stress of the day drifting away. Rinn stayed in front of them, not looking back.

When they reached the bottom, her master turned her to face him and stepped back.

"Now, as is custom, I must ask for your amulet. For the next seven days you will have only the power which you were born with. When Jalthrax is ready, you will begin practicing with *real* dragon magic."

Elody brought her hands to the amulet hugging her neck. She took it in her fingers and grudgingly began to lift the chain off her breast. She stopped and let it fall back.

"Without the amulet, I have only enough power to cast simple cantrips, if even that," she said. "I have never even tried to cast without it."

"You will have Jalthrax by your side soon enough, and you will know more power than you have ever known from the amulet. You will not need your magic for the next seven days. Your focus will be on Jalthrax and bonding with him. You need no more magic for that."

She started to move her hand and hesitated again. The master smiled knowingly and put his hand on her shoulder.

"You have grown to depend on your magic, yes?"

She nodded sheepishly.

"The amulet has served as the source of your power throughout your years of training, and you have been one of my finest pupils in the study of magic. But the power you wield is not your own. We do not possess that kind of power in ourselves. Jalthrax will give that power freely of himself, you will see."

"Besides," her brother said, "you still have power without the amulet. I can still cast spells. If I cared to."

The master glared at him, and Rinn locked eyes defiantly.

"You were my greatest disappointment," he said flatly.

He snapped his head back to Elody and did not look at Rinn again. Elody watched Rinn turn and walk down the path away from the two of them and waited until he was out of earshot to speak.

"You are too hard on him, Master. It is not his fault his dragon didn't bond."

"He spent more time chasing girls than at his studies. If he had studied his spells and cast them properly, the bond would have taken."

The master grabbed the reins of a horse tied to a small tree at the base of the mountain. As he spoke, he pulled the horse onto the path.

"He knows that he is partly to blame," she said.

"He is completely to blame."

Elody said nothing else. The master stopped in front of her and beckoned her to come forward. She sighed and removed the amulet from around her neck, handing it over to the master with a turn of her head so that she didn't have to watch him take it.

"You will be fine, my dear. Practice your cantrips. It is only seven days."

He put his arm around her and pulled her onto the trail alongside him. Rinn fell quietly into step behind them. A ways behind them.

***

They walked together in the shadow of the great mountain. The trees that edged the path had dropped many leaves onto it, nearly choking it from sight in places. She heard Rinn crunching through leaves as loudly as he could behind her. Her master did not speak again as they walked, but she caught him smiling at her several times.

"Is my training done, Master?"

"Your training will never be done. Not until the day you leave this world. Your time with me, however, is at an end. I do not teach dragonmages."

Elody stared down at the ground a while before looking back up. She caught him smiling at her again, but he held her gaze when their eyes met. He reached his hand down and gently patted her shoulder.

"You will be a fine dragonmage, my dear."

She smiled back at him and pulled her shoulders up a little. They trudged the path that went along the base of the mountain and followed it back to the main road. Elody looked back a couple of times to see her brother looking down and kicking rocks and leaves along the ground.

The mountain path came to an abrupt end where it joined the main road, and they all silently turned south toward their village. After a few minutes along the road, Elody turned to see that Rinn had stopped and was looking back. She tapped her master's shoulder and pointed to where she saw a man on horseback coming up behind them.

He turned around and handed the reins to Elody as he quickly moved past Rinn.

"Stay behind me," he said to them both.

He stepped in front of Rinn and put his hand to the side to signal him to step back as well. Elody walked up beside her brother, and they both took a few steps forward to stand beside her master. Rinn pulled the knife on his belt with one hand and pushed her back a bit with the other.

"Put that away," the master said.

Rinn lowered his hand to his side but did not return the knife to its sheath. They all stood silently, watching the man's approach. As he got closer, Elody could see the dull grey of his mail armor draped down his chest and flowing down over his legs in the saddle. Her master walked forward a few steps and then stopped. He watched cautiously and then smiled.

"Ho there, good knight," he said.

"Ho there," the man called back.

She saw her master smile again, and the man smiled back. As the man got nearer she could see that his horse, too, had armor across its head. He rode tall in the saddle and kept his body perfectly straight as he approached.

"It's okay, Rinn," she said, stepping forward. "He's a knight."

"Because he has armor and a horse?" he said, pulling her back again. "What if he killed a knight and stole them?"

She looked to her brother and back up to watch the man's approach. He rode perfectly at ease with his hand gently on the reins. A longsword hung at his belt and slapped lightly against his leg as he rode. He caught her eye and smiled at her with a nod of his head.

"What brings you out this way, sir?" her master said.

"The knights have sent me to these lands to watch over its people."

"I am Cythyil," her master said.

"Berym," the knight replied.

"Well met, Sir Berym."

"Just Berym," the knight said as he climbed down out of his saddle.

Elody saw Rinn eyeing the knight. He had stepped in front of her to keep her to the back, but she did a quick step around him, handing the reins to him as she did. Without taking her eyes from the man, she gave Rinn's hand that was holding his knife a light slap, and he tucked it back into his belt.

"Hi. I'm Elody."

The knight smiled and bowed, even waving his hand in a flourish as he went down. His eyes never left hers.

"Young lady," he said.

Elody smiled back at him and tried to hide her red cheeks.

"Where are you headed, sir?" her master asked.

"To Jornath."

"That's where we live!" Elody said.

Rinn grabbed her robe and pulled her back a bit.

"We don't need a knight for anything," Rinn said.

"Of course not, and glad I am for it. You are Elody's brother?"

"Rinn."

"Well met, Rinn. It's a good man that watches after his little sister."

The knight bowed again but more formally. Rinn straightened himself in response and nodded.

"If there is no work for my sword," the knight said, "I

shall work the fields. Or gather firewood. Or repair houses. Not all of a knight's work is done with a blade."

"Rinn is right," Cythyil said, "there's not much call for a knight in Jornath. It's a small village. They do not have even a tavern or inn. Just a few small shops."

"That is where my travels take me, and so that is where I shall go."

Cythyil thought for a second, and his eyes brightened.

"Well, then perhaps you could help me. I had planned to walk the children back home before returning to my own village, but it adds several hours to my trip. Could I trouble you to walk them to the village?"

"The *children* will be just fine without either of you," Rinn said.

"I have no doubt of it," said the knight. "But perhaps you could show me the way for my own sake?"

"Sure, we can show you!" Elody said.

Rinn threw her an annoyed glance, but she just ignored it. Cythyil turned to her and smiled.

"This is where we part ways, my dear. You will come and visit me, yes?"

"Of course, Master."

"Tut tut. I am your master no longer. You may call me Cythyil from now on."

Elody smiled and took a deep breath, pushing her chest out a bit as she did. She pulled herself up tall and held her hand out to him. He smiled back and took it in a firm handshake before placing his other hand over hers and loosening his grip.

"Thank you for everything, Master."

He tugged her hand and gave her a playful, stern look.

"I mean Cythyil," she said as she stood taller still.

He gave her hand one last little shake before taking the reins from Rinn without looking at him. Cythyil turned back to the knight and gave a little bow.

"Well met, Sir Berym."

"Well met, Cythyil" the knight said.

Cythyil mounted his horse without another word and rode off down the north road into the mountains. Elody watched him a moment longer before turning back to see her brother eyeing the knight. The knight's only answer was to smile back.

"We'd better get going. Rinn, will you lead the way?" the knight asked, grabbing the reins of his horse.

Rinn straightened up again and turned south down the main road. Elody watched as he walked in front of them a few paces, his legs moving more stiffly as though he were marching. She looked up at the knight walking beside her, and he winked down at her. She looked ahead at her brother and a big grin spread across her face.

"I've never met a knight before," Elody said.

"Have none come to your village since the war?"

"A few when I was little, but they never stay long. I guess we don't have much to stick around for."

"We help where we can, but we are sometimes called away to help those in greater need. It is a good thing the knights never stayed long. It meant your village was safe and there was no reason for them to stay."

"Our village is still safe," Rinn said over his shoulder.

"Let us hope so," the knight said. "I have traveled from Havnor, and I've heard tell of goblins along the road and in the forest, though I have seen none for myself."

"Oh! Our aunt lives in Havnor!" Elody said. "She's a witch there."

"Goblin attacks are pretty common out here," Rinn said. "We manage to do just fine without knights coming to our rescue."

"Yes, I can see that," Berym said. He looked down at Elody and smiled. "I am in Havnor quite a lot these days. Once I leave Jornath, I will go to Buxbaum for a few days, and then back to Havnor. If you would like, I can deliver a message to your aunt for you."

"That's okay. We see her every fall when she comes in for High Harvest."

"That sounds wonderful. I wish I could stay long enough to enjoy it."

"Why are you coming to Jornath?" Elody asked.

"It was time. The knights are spread all across Gondril, but we try to make regular visits to every village when we can."

"We haven't seen a knight in years," her brother called back.

"We *try* to make regular visits," the knight said, "but sometimes more time passes than we would like. The talk of goblins became too frequent to ignore."

"We haven't seen a goblin in years either," Rinn called back.

"Nor have I, truth be told, but the news floating up north speaks of trouble. Some of the smaller villages on the outskirts of the settled lands, like yours, don't get the attention they need. Some villages have a dragonmage, but most cannot afford one. But tell me now, Elody, such fine robes are an odd thing for a girl your age to wear. Are you a dragonmage?"

"Yes, I am!"

"Dragonmage *in training*," her brother called back.

She waved her arm at him as if to shoo him away.

"My dragon was just born today!"

"Born just today? That is exciting! Where did you train? Surely not in your small village."

"Oh, no. I trained with master Cythyil in Baglund."

"Baglund? That's quite a journey to take every day."

"Rinn would take me and leave me. Master Cythyil took me in as a boarder during the weeks that I would train, and Rinn would come back every few weeks to take me home."

"That's a lot of travel," Berym said.

"Cythyil is the closest master to our village," Elody said. "It was very generous of him to take us in."

Berym nodded.

"So tell me about your new dragon!" he said.

"His name is Jalthrax, and he's the most beautiful dragon I've ever seen!"

Elody talked incessantly about Jalthrax the rest of the way home. Rinn looked back over his shoulder a few times to catch Berym's eye, but the knight only winked at him before turning back to Elody with a smile.

CHAPTER TWO

FLIGHT

ERYNINN DOVE BEHIND the trunk of a huge tree as several crude arrows sailed past. He heard one thunk into the tree behind his head and said a silent prayer of thanks to no god in particular. He didn't need to count his arrows, but he reached his hand back anyway.

Six arrows left.

And a lot more goblins.

He could hear them yelling at each other in their guttural language as he hid behind his tree and weighed his options. A quick glance with his sharp, elven eyes caught them flitting from tree to tree and gathering closer. They crept slowly out and started walking in a wide line toward him.

He pulled four arrows from his quiver and stuck them into the ground in a line in front of him. Taking a deep breath, he stepped out from behind the tree and called out to them in goblin.

"Filthy beast!"

It was the only goblin he knew. His mother would

call him that in the crude language when he would come home muddy and dirty. It wasn't the greatest of insults, but it had the intended effect.

Four arrows flew at him from the goblin archers, but he was already dodging back behind the tree. He heard two more arrows sink into the trunk. Nocking an arrow, he pulled the string back and rolled around. Taking only a second to aim at the small group of archers, he loosed. He moved back behind the tree before it hit, but he heard a loud scream and several howls that put a smile on his lips.

Five arrows left.

He peeked again and then rolled back as he heard more bowstrings twang. Two more arrows sailed past and another thunked into the trunk behind him. Stepping back around with another arrow, he saw them scatter as he came into sight. He drew back and aimed at another of the archers and shot him in the back. He tumbled forward and lay still.

Four arrows left.

The goblins were in a panic now, but another brave archer turned back and drew his bow to shoot. Eryninn was faster. Nocking another arrow, he put it through the goblin's chest, killing him before he could even draw his arm back. Brave, but not smart.

Three arrows left.

The other goblins were in complete disarray, howling at one another and stumbling over each other to try and get away from the deadly arrows. Eryninn let a little smile creep through at the scene, but it quickly disappeared when the last archer loosed an arrow that just missed his head. His look of surprise quickly turned into a glare as he nocked and shot another arrow. The creature squealed and ran, ducking behind a tree as the arrow sailed past.

"Damn."

Two arrows left.

The rest of the goblins scrambled around behind cover for a bit, but he could not play this game forever. The longer he stayed hidden, the more courage they gained. Even now he could hear them calling out to each other and forming a plan. He couldn't just stand there and let them plot his doom.

Eryninn ran.

He heard whoops and shouts behind him as the rest of the goblins burst from cover and took up the chase. He pulled an arrow as he ran, nocked it, and turned around with a hapless shot that was only meant to scatter them. It worked. They all went diving for cover, but they were back up in moments and resuming their pursuit.

One arrow left.

His hand fell to the shortsword on his hip. Even at a distance he could see the swords and long spears the goblins wielded. Despite his well-placed shots, there were still too many of them. He wouldn't be much of a match for them in a sword fight if it came to that.

"Damn."

Eryninn ran faster.

The goblins charged and hollered again, with a little

less enthusiasm this time, but they got louder with each step. He wouldn't be able to outrun them. They were too small and nimble, and he was losing strength the longer he kept up the pace. His eyes darted around for a place he might hide. He glanced over his shoulder and saw the goblins had come together and were running in a pack behind him.

Eryninn had hoped his arrows would scare them enough to leave off their pursuit. He could hear them catching up behind him, and their shouts were louder and more furious with each passing second. His legs were getting tired. He pulled his last arrow and stopped long enough to shoot it clumsily. It sailed harmlessly over their heads. None even stopped to duck this time.

No more arrows.

He had some strength left to keep running, but he would not escape his pursuers. He drew his shortsword and began swinging it around him in a grand display. He twirled it left and right over his shoulders and shifted from one hand to the other showing off all of his fancy moves. He yelled loudly with all of his might and tried to stand up and look menacing.

The goblins slowed their charge and watched with wary eyes. At least half a dozen he could see. They stood in silence and watched his theatrics before looking to each other and then turning back to him with a grin.

"Damn."

He was no slouch with a blade, but he would not win this fight. He continued to spin his shortsword in sweeping circles that kept the goblins from rushing all at once, but their fear would most certainly be shorter-lived than his stamina.

The goblins crept closer.

One of them hurled a spear at him, but he easily skipped out of its path where it buried itself into the ground a few steps behind him. He stepped back until he felt his foot brush against it and then pulled it out of the dirt. Switching his blade to his left hand, he picked it up over his shoulder and chucked it back at them.

The goblins jumped to the sides to avoid the spear, but it had little chance of hitting them to begin with. He couldn't have hit with the crude spear even if he had wanted to, but the distraction was enough. The little creatures turned back as one to face him only to find he was already on top of them.

Eryninn slashed out with his shortsword, cutting one across the chest before it had the chance to register where he was. He stabbed it in the gut and kicked it to the ground. The rest of the goblins quickly regained their bearings and charged in together. They lunged with their swords.

Eryninn got his sword up in time to parry the clumsy attacks, but the assault forced him back a few steps. He swung his shortsword in a long arc in front of him, pushing them back as well. He used the small bit of breathing room to skip back a few steps and try and come up with a plan of attack. He had to think of something.

Nothing came to mind.

The goblins charged in again. Eryninn knocked

several of their blades away, but one got through and stabbed him in the side. It wasn't a deep cut, but it was enough. He cried out in pain. The goblins squealed in delight and drove in harder. He pressed his hand to his side and clenched his teeth.

"Damn!"

Eryninn backpedaled as fast as he could, but they were right there on him. He held his hand to his side and felt the warm blood from the wound seeping through his shirt. With as much determination as he could muster, he stood up straight and gripped his sword with both hands.

The goblins came in for another strike, but he stepped back quickly out of their reach. They were small and nimble, but their swords were short, and their arms even shorter. As their swings passed harmlessly in front of him he charged in with a yell.

He slashed one across the stomach, cutting it open as it screeched and stumbled back. The other goblins closed in as he stabbed out, catching another in the side. He was putting up a good fight, but he could feel the blood pouring down his leg in a constant reminder of the death that pulled at him.

The remaining goblins skipped back away from his deadly sword and held their guard. He stood there, silently thankful for the respite, even if it was only for a moment. They waited there, staring at him. One said something to the others. Eryninn didn't understand their language, but the toothy grins on their faces said everything. He looked down at the blood they were eyeing at his side and knew their plan.

Just wait for me to fall.

Eryninn tightened the grip on his sword and leapt forward, stabbing at them. He stumbled. Or at least he looked like he stumbled. He smiled to himself as the goblins laughed and lunged forward. He crouched down and swung his back leg forward in a sweeping arc. None of them saw it coming. He swept their legs out from under them, knocking them all to the ground.

Then Eryninn ran.

Leaving them rolling around in a mass of flailing arms and legs, he jumped up and ran as fast as he could. His side throbbed and gushed blood, and the muscles in his legs screamed in protest, but he ran for his life. He heard the goblins shouting and cursing as they stood from the heap and picked up the chase again.

His only hope now was to outrun them and hide.

CHAPTER THREE

AN AUDIENCE WITH THE QUEEN

ELODY CONCENTRATED AS hard as she could. Her eyes were closed and her face was tight and trembling with effort. She focused all of her thoughts inward, trying to find the tiny well of magic she knew was inside of her. She even pulled her hands up from the pit of her stomach as though she were trying to physically lift it out of her.

Nothing happened.

"Dammit!"

Her whole body shook, and her fists went white. She wanted to scream. She had been trying for an hour to find her magic, but she had met with limited success. She opened her eyes and threw up her hands. On the verge of tears, she stomped across the yard and plopped down on a tree stump. She was breathing heavily from the exertion as she dropped her face into her hands and sighed.

It's too hard.

Why did they take her amulet away? She couldn't

even do simple cantrips now. Elody had spent very little time in school testing her own magic. Even when she was supposed to be, she rarely did. Her amulet provided more than enough magic. My time was better spent learning spells.

"You're on my stump."

Elody picked her head up and blocked the sun with her hand as she stared at her brother. He folded his arms and pointed to where she was seated.

"Unless you want us all to freeze at the first frost, I need to chop wood," he said.

Elody got up without a word and walked over to the other side of the yard. She looked back to see Rinn watching her. Does he have to be here? With her back to him, she closed her eyes and breathed deeply, trying to calm herself. She stood motionless and tried to focus her thoughts, but the sharp crack of splitting wood broke her concentration.

"I'm trying to practice!" she shouted. "Can't you do that some other time?"

"So practice," he said. "I'm not stopping you."

She whirled around and glared at him, but he only smiled and swung the axe down, splitting another log in two.

"I'll tell Dad you're bothering me!"

"Who do you think told me to chop the damn wood?"

She huffed and turned away. She shook her hands and slung them as though she were flinging water off of them. She closed her eyes and forced herself to breathe slowly. Deep breaths. Focus. She managed to calm herself when she heard a whisper in her ear.

"When are you going to start practicing?"

She spun around, leading with her fist to slug her brother, but he was nowhere near her. She looked up to see him standing all the way across the yard. His axe was resting on the stump, and his arms were folded with a giant grin on his face.

"How did you do that?" she asked.

"I may not have a dragon, but I still have as much training as you do."

"But how did you do it? How did you summon the magic?"

A little smile crept across his face.

"You can't do it, can you?"

"Shut up and show me!"

"I've always been more powerful than you," he said.

She opened her mouth to scream a protest, but she couldn't. He's right. He has always been better with magic. With a sigh, Elody dropped her chin to her chest and clenched her eyes. Her shoulders bounced as she sobbed silently.

"Oh, for Threyl's sake!" he said. "Is that your answer for everything?"

She slumped even more as she tried hard to be silent and turned her back to him.

"Oh, for... You can feel it in you, right?"

She bobbed her head without looking up, but she could hear him walking across the yard.

"Well, think of it like this little well inside of you. It's small. At least it is for me. You'll feel it when you find it. Imagine your hands dipping into it and then holding it in your palm and between your fingers. Does that make sense?"

She nodded and looked up as she turned back around. She wiped her puffy, red eyes on her sleeve.

"The master once told me that when you have a dragon, it's like dipping your hands into a fast river," he said. "You can almost feel the magic flowing through your fingers, and you just take as much as you need. But the well of magic in *us* is small, like a muddy rain puddle. You have to coax it out carefully, and there's only a little to take. Now. Close your eyes."

She wiped her eyes again and closed them.

"Can you feel it? Like it's in your chest or your stomach."

She took a deep breath and thought. She nodded.

"Imagine dipping your hands into it like you're going to drink from a barrel. Cup it in your hands and bring it up slowly. Keep your fingers together."

Elody breathed deeply and tried to block out the sensations around her. She thought of her hands reaching into her stomach and brought her own hands up and spread her fingers over her abdomen. She clenched her eyes shut and pushed up with her hands. Still nothing happened.

She opened her eyes and screamed, throwing her hands into the air.

"Stop, stop!" Rinn said. "You can't lose focus. This is your first time without an amulet. It's not easy at first.

Close your eyes again."

She folded her arms and stared at him.

"I'm trying to help you," he said.

She dropped her hands to her side with a sigh and closed her eyes again.

"Think of a bowl of water," Rinn said. "It's just sitting there, all blue and sparkly. And you reach your hand down toward it and then just touch it. Feel it between your fingertips. Curl your fingers into a cup and dip them slowly in. You'll feel it in your hands. You'll feel that tingle in your fingers just like using the amulet."

Elody took a deep breath. She focused her mind and imagined her fingers gently reaching down. She felt a tiny spark of something deep in the pit of her stomach and pushed her imaginary fingers toward it. She could feel it pulling away from her, but she pushed her mind deeper and deeper. She felt something. It was as if her fingers touched something cold. Her eyes shot open, and the feeling left her instantly.

"See?" Rinn said. "Close your eyes."

Elody tried to keep a smile from her face as she closed her eyes. She reached down again and touched the magic within her. It was easier to find this time. She felt her fingers, her actual fingers, start to tingle with a sensation that was both familiar and foreign at the same time. She could hear Rinn whispering through her concentration.

"You've got it. Now hold it and take it."

She pulled her hands up from her waist and toward her chest. She could feel the magic flow down her palms and into her fingertips as she brought them higher. In her mind, the cold blue magic pooled in her hands. She felt somehow that she had just enough for her spell.

Elody opened her eyes slowly and started to move her hands. She took the magic from within her and began to weave it into her spell using the motions she had practiced for years. Her fingers floated through delicate, intricate movements, and she could feel the tingling sensation building.

As her hands and fingers danced through the motions, she could feel the tiny wisps of magic leap from one to the next. It was less than she was accustomed to with her amulet, but it was enough. Weaving the strands together, she shaped it to her needs.

She could feel the magic almost leap from her hands as she finished the spell. It sprang from her finger as she pointed at a bucket a few feet away. With a graceful flick of her wrist, the bucket floated off the ground and hovered in the air. She turned her hand over with a pulling motion, and it moved slowly through the air toward her.

Her eyes sparkled as she smiled at Rinn who just rolled his eyes.

"Anyone can lift a bucket," he said.

Her face dropped right along with the bucket, and they both flinched as it clattered to the ground.

"You're so mean!" she shouted.

"I just meant you're going to have to do a lot better than that so that maybe one day you can protect yourself, and I don't have to anymore."

"I don't need your protection! I can take care of myself just fine!"

"I still have more power than you. I can cast more than just cantrips without ever having known a dragon. You go ahead and float your buckets around. You can't do more than that without your dragon."

He turned back and picked up his axe.

"At least I have a dragon."

He froze in place.

She closed her eyes and reached inside of her for the magic. She found it almost immediately this time, and she started pulling at it, collecting it in her hands. She began weaving them, this time at a faster pace. The spell was still just a simple cantrip, but it was more complicated than the one she had just cast. As she opened her eyes a crack, she could see her brother turn back to watch her. He stared at her curiously, trying to discern the pattern she was weaving, but he realized too late what was happening.

A flash of light burst from her hands, and a loud bang split the air. Rinn tried to throw his hands up, but he couldn't block it. He stumbled back and fell to the ground, stunned and dazed.

"Hey!"

Elody looked up with a satisfied smile to see her father hurrying across the yard. His forehead was creased, and his eyes were narrow, and he was looking right at her. Her smile disappeared. Her brother was just regaining his senses and standing up when her father reached them both.

"I don't ever want to see that again! Do you think this is all for fun?"

Rinn managed to get to his feet and scurried away from his sister. Elody shook her head and dropped her eyes.

"You're not careful with that stuff, and you're liable to get one or both of you killed some day!"

He stared at her and waited for her to meet his eyes.

"Rinn, go around the house and get the hogs ready. We'll take 'em out to the woods as soon as I'm done here."

Rinn left without a word. Elody picked her head up and held her father's gaze with a look of angry defiance, but she knew she was wrong. Her father put his hands on his hips and shook his head.

"You're as bad as your mother."

His mouth cracked in a smile, and she couldn't help but smile back.

"Gave your brother quite a shock, I bet."

She started laughing, and he smiled.

"I'm sorry, Daddy."

"I know, little girl. He probably deserved it."

He chuckled again and then shook his head.

"You have to control yourself and your magic, or it can do more harm than good. Your mama always told me that."

She nodded her head as he pulled her in and put his arms around her. She closed her eyes and laid her head on his chest.

"She woulda been proud to see you."

She opened her eyes and pulled away from him.

"Not if she saw what I just did."

"Well, she was known for a few pranks in her days too."

"I have so much to learn still."

"She never achieved what you have. She woulda been proud to see all you've done."

He pulled her back to him and put an arm around her.

"I can't wait for you to meet Jalthrax, Dad! He's so amazing!"

"I can't wait."

She smiled as he let her go and held her at arms length. He looked her up and down just long enough to make her blush before he let her go. With a chuckle and a sigh he smiled back at her.

"Hey, listen. Don't go into town for a while. I'm not supposed to tell you, but the whole town is planning a big thing for you."

Elody blushed.

"They don't have to do that."

"They know that. I tried to talk 'em out of it, but they wouldn't listen. They paid a lot of money for your training, and they're all proud of you. They've been waiting five years for this little village to have a dragonmage."

"I've only been training for three years, Dad."

"They've been waitin' longer than that, love."

She started to ask when she realized what he meant. She looked down as she spoke.

"I don't want a party. I don't want to hurt Rinn like that."

"They're proud of you, Elody. They want to show you that, and you can't stop 'em. I'll talk with Rinn."

She looked back up with a tiny smile. He winked at her and walked off around the house. Once he was out of sight she closed her eyes and took a deep breath.

***

It was just before lunch when Elody finished practicing. She gathered up the rabbits her father had trapped and left for her and put them in her pack. She left the yard and started the trek to the cave north of the village that held her beloved Jalthrax.

It was her third time to make the trip, but from the very first day she could feel that her love for the little dragon was stronger than she had realized. She thought of him like her own baby, yet he was so far from helpless. She couldn't wait to see him every day, and she really couldn't wait to bring him home.

Elody skirted the west edge of the village and turned north into the woods and toward the mountains. She knew that it would take over an hour to reach the cave, but her load was light and her steps even lighter. She even started skipping as a smile crossed her face.

The village was long out of sight when she felt someone watching her. She stopped skipping but kept moving at the same pace. She spun around and scanned the trees but saw nothing. With a shrug to herself, she kept walking.

She heard something and stopped. Now she knew

someone was there. She whirled around again and brought her hands up, though she didn't think she had enough magic left in her to actually cast anything.

"Show yourself!" she said.

She waited another breathless minute for something, anything, to move and reveal itself. Then she heard a whisper on the wind in her ear.

"There's no one here. Keep skipping."

"Rinn!"

Rinn stepped out from behind the tree where he was hiding with a big grin splayed across his face.

"Sorry," he said. "I really liked the skipping. It reminds me that you're still my little sister."

"What are you doing here?"

"Making sure you're safe."

"I'm going to see Jalthrax just like I've done for the past two days. I'm perfectly safe."

"I know, and I've followed you both days."

"You've been following me? I don't want you following me!"

"There are goblins out here, Elody. Gald said he's seen signs of them in the forest. You need someone to protect you."

"I don't need anyone to protect me, and I've never seen any goblins out here."

"You don't see much of anything. I've been following you for days, and this is the first you've caught wind of it. If I had been a goblin, you'd be dead already. That is, of course, unless you had a big brother watching your back."

"I'm telling Dad when we get home."

"Dad's the one who told me to follow you."

Elody narrowed her eyes and scrunched her face. Of course he did. That's just something her father would do. Ever since her mother had died, and even before, Dad had tasked Rinn with being her protector.

When she turned twelve and was sent to Cythyil to train as a dragonmage, her father had sent Rinn along every week to take her and then again to bring her home. He hated it. She knew he hated it. Having to drop her off at the front gate of the school. The constant reminder of his failure.

Rinn had always been there.

But she was fifteen now. She had been practicing magic for three years in the hopes of getting a dragon. Though she no longer had the amulet that gave her the power to cast all those years, she still had some power. Enough to cast spells to keep her safe. *I don't need protection anymore. I have Jalthrax now.*

"I don't care what Dad says," Elody said. "I don't need you to protect me. Go home."

"Nope. I'll stay back and out of your way. I'll even sneak behind trees if you want to pretend I'm not here, but on Dad's orders, and because you're my little sister whether you like it or not, I'm not going home."

Elody crossed her arms over her chest and glared at him with everything her fifteen-year-old face could muster. Rinn just returned the look with a grin.

"Fine," she said. "Come if you want, but don't go anywhere near the cave."

"I'll wait at the bottom," he said.

She whirled back around and started off down the trail without looking back to see if her brother was following. She knew that he was. He was always behind her somewhere.

The trail was well worn. It led north to the base of the smaller mountains beneath Ilothen's Crown where it turned east and toward the rest of civilization. The range was known as the Twin Crest Mountains, named for the two twin mountains that towered over all others.

Ilothen's Crown was said to be the tallest mountain in all of Gondril. Looking up and up, Elody believed it. She had lived her whole life in its shadow. It gave her comfort to look up and see its watchful summit, always covered with snow, looking down on her.

Her destination today, though, was the smaller mountains beneath the Crown. The short mountain closest to Jornath was where the Silver Queen made her home. The trail from the main road that led through this part of the forest turned west, toward the low peak.

It wasn't a long journey. In another hour they reached the bottom. Their eyes stared at the long path that twisted up the mountainside to the silver dragon's cave. Elody sighed. I hate this part.

"I'll wait here," Rinn said.

"I might be a while."

"I know. I'll be here."

Without looking back, she started the long walk up the mountain. It took her another half hour to climb the path and reach the entrance of the cave. As she had done in the days past, she called out into the cave.

"Silver Queen? It's Elody. May I enter?"

She heard the melodic, beastly voice echo off the cave walls.

"You may enter."

She smiled and walked into the cave. She strode in confidently with her pack across her back and peered around, excited to catch her first glimpse of Jalthrax.

As Elody rounded the corner into the main cavern, she was greeted with the awe-inspiring sight of the Silver Queen stretched to her full height. She stood on all four of her giant claws, and her wings were stretched out, reaching all the way to the walls of the cave. She had never seen a dragon that big. She felt a lump in her throat.

So enraptured was she by the sight that it took a moment to realize that she didn't see Jalthrax anywhere. She pulled her eyes away and scanned the cavern, but there was no sign of him. Then a movement high in the tall cavern, gliding around his birthmother's head, caught her eye.

Jalthrax was flying.

"He can fly?" she yelled.

The Silver Queen nodded and smiled her familiar smile.

"I didn't know they could fly so soon."

"He could fly within hours of his birth. This is only the first time you've seen it. Jalthrax is a very strong boy."

"He's amazing!"

Her voice seemed small in the giant cavern, but even with his wings flapping and the wind rushing past his ears, Jalthrax heard her. With a screech of excitement, he banked to the right in a tight loop and glided to the ground.

As soon as his claws touched, he rushed toward Elody who was still standing stunned at how graceful her little dragon looked in flight. She couldn't believe that he had learned to fly and, more importantly, land in such a short time. He was still only three days old.

He swished his tail, kicking up dirt, as he rushed to meet her. She dropped to her knees and threw her arms around his long neck and gave him a squeeze.

"Hey, Sweet Boy. I missed you. Are you hungry?"

Elody pulled the pack off her back and started pulling rabbits out and tossing them to him. He snaked his neck and grabbed each one out of the air as they flew, piling them in front of him. Then he laid down and started eating them one by one.

Elody looked up again as the Silver Queen lowered her bulky frame to the ground and then slowly laid her head down on the cave floor and curled close to her body. She watched her son tear apart each rabbit as he ate and smiled.

"He is a hungry boy," she said. "He has already hunted this morning, yet still he eats more. In time he will not need to eat every day, but for now he is young and growing."

This was the first time that the Silver Queen had really spoken to her other than their official greeting and the occasional pleasantry. Even the master spoke only formally to her. It was not common for dragonmages to speak so familiarly to an unkept dragon, especially not a dragon mother. At least, I don't think so.

"I have already begun teaching him the language of our kind."

"They can learn to speak at this age?"

"Your tone continues to carry surprise. Jalthrax is not a hound. He is not your pet to feed and care for. I should dare say that though his mind is not but a few days old, he already possesses more innate intelligence than you."

"I am sorry, Silver Queen. We spend our time in school learning the magic and how to handle our dragons. Only a few weeks in our earliest years are spent learning about the dragons themselves. I meant no offense or to imply that Jalthrax is anything other than special to me."

The great dragon eyed her briefly and then lowered her gaze.

"I should not have been so abrupt with you," she said. "Your master should teach you more about my kind. It is a pity that you would seek to use my son to further your own power without bothering to spend the time to learn what it is you use."

"I'm sorry, Silver Queen. I was told that dragonmages learn all they need to know of dragons once they actually bond with one."

The Silver Queen sighed and nodded her head and said no more. The silence dragged on, broken only by the sound of tearing flesh and crunching bone as Jalthrax devoured his meal. Elody felt so uncomfortable that she reached out and started rubbing his head just so she had something to do with her hands. Then she suddenly thought that she was treating him like a dog and jerked her hand back.

"It's all right to touch him," the Silver Queen said. "All manner of creatures, even ones as large as dragons, like the sensation of being touched. Stroke your hand down his neck."

Elody reached out tentatively and placed her hand on the side of Jalthrax's neck. By this time he had finished his meal and was watching Elody with wide-eyed interest. She rubbed her hand down his neck and down the side of his body. She felt a low rumble in his body as he growled in pleasure and jerked her hand back.

Jalthrax snapped his eyes open and looked at her. She stared into his eyes and saw what his birthmother meant. She saw not the eyes of a dog or a beast. It's like he knows me already. He regarded her with his head cocked and then opened his mouth and let out a little screech. She jumped in surprise and laughed. The Silver Queen chuckled as well, an eerie growl that sounded like stone scraping on stone.

Elody continued to stroke Jalthrax's neck. She had so many questions, but she didn't want to look foolish in front of the Silver Queen, so she just kept her mouth shut.

"He loves you, you know."

Elody looked into the Silver Queen's silver eyes and kept rubbing her hand down Jalthrax's neck.

"He is yours, forever more. He will know me as his birthmother, but he will not love me as he loves you. That is the bond you have formed."

"May I ask you a question, Silver Queen?"

The big dragon nodded her head with a gentle smile.

"Did you have any that you kept from this clutch? We learned that a dragon mother often keeps one egg as her own to raise."

"That clutch was over two years ago, and I laid only one egg that year, which is rare for my kind. But I have never kept one of my children. I have given them all to young mages like you."

Elody thought silently, trying to think of how to ask her next question.

"You want to know why, yes?"

Elody smiled sheepishly.

"Yes."

"I did not wish to raise a child of my own right now. I have a long time to decide when I will raise my own children. Dragons live very long lives."

"Yes, some almost a millennium," Elody said proudly but then felt foolish for interrupting.

"Some longer than that," the Silver Queen said. "When a female reaches breeding age, she can lay a clutch of eggs every year she chooses. But raising a child is a much bigger commitment than simply giving away your eggs. Before the dragonmages discovered their abilities to bond with our offspring, most mothers of my kind would simply choose not to mate. Some years, I still choose not to."

"But why do you do it? Why do you give up your young for us?"

"Sweet child. I am giving up but a tiny portion of Jalthrax's life to you. You will not even live to see a single century, yet he will likely live more than eight hundred years in perfect health. Some of my kind have been known to live over a millennia."

Elody blinked.

A thousand years? The master never told her that a dragon could live that long. She looked down at the little body that was now nuzzling his neck into her hand. She would not live to see even a tiny amount of his long life. Her next words caught in her throat.

"When I die, will he... will he be old enough for a family?"

"He will be as you are now. Barely an adult. He may just be old enough to find a mate of his own when you are gone. So you see child, we do not give up the lives of our children for your kind. We give but a tiny bit of their time."

"Do all the dragons of light give to dragonmages?"

"Only a small few. You call us the dragon mothers. There are some of my kind that believe we give away our children to the undeserving, but we are all free to do as we choose. This is the choice I have made."

"Do the dark dragons give up their eggs as well?"

"Some do. Most of them abandon their nests after laying eggs. The dark dragons are not blessed with Anarr's light and wisdom. Most rarely stay to raise their young. Those who seek power from our children can often find it lying in wait for them to simply pick it up."

"They don't raise their own children? Maybe that's

why they grow up to be so bad."

The great dragon smiled and chuckled.

"Perhaps so."

"But the dragons of light stay with their children?"

"Dragons are born with the ability to defend and hunt for themselves, so it is not necessary for the mother or father to remain. Most dragons of light do, though. It is our responsibility to teach our children and protect them into young adulthood just as your kind does."

"How long have you been a dragon mother?"

"I gave my first egg over a decade ago, right in this very cave."

"How many eggs have you given since then?"

"Eighteen."

"Do you remember them all?"

The big dragon cocked her head at the question.

"Of course I do. The seven days we spend with our children is for more than just their safety. In seven days, I must impart to my children all that they will need to begin their life. I must form my own bond as their birthmother. Yes, I remember all of my children."

Elody grew silent again. She had more questions, but she felt like she was asking too many.

"You have more questions. Ask them."

"Were you a bonded dragon, Silver Queen?"

"I was. Most dragon mothers were bonded at one time. The ones who never bond don't understand what it means to be so. I was bonded for more than two centuries."

Elody looked at her in surprise.

"Then your bonded parent was an elf?"

"Yes. Most silver and gold dragons are given to the elves. They are the only race that can live long enough to see our kind into old age."

"So why give your children to humans when the silver dragons are usually given to the elves."

"Because when you die, Jalthrax will have a long, long life ahead of him to forget you."

Elody looked down and bit her lip.

"Does that bother you to hear that?"

Elody shook her head but couldn't look up.

"Jalthrax will love you until the day that you die and for many, many years after. But he will only be with you for a short time in his life. When a dragon is given to an elf, they will spend sometimes their whole lives with their bonded parent. It is much harder to go on without them when they are gone."

"Is… that what happened to you?"

The old dragon let her eyes slip down and close.

"I'm tired now, child. You will come again tomorrow."

Elody sat confused for a moment and then stood to leave. Jalthrax, too, had fallen asleep while she was stroking his neck, so she touched him one last time to say goodbye and then left.

Elody walked down the mountain and past her brother who was sitting on a rock at the base and twirling his dagger in his hand. He jumped up as she marched by.

"Hey! I caught a rabbit. One throw."

He gripped his dagger by the blade and snapped his

arm out to demonstrate.

"Stuck it right to the ground. I figured maybe you could give it to Jalthrax tomorrow."

He sheathed his dagger and held a rabbit toward her, but she just kept walking. He caught up to her and started asking a bunch of questions as they walked. Elody just walked quietly without answering until her brother got the hint and shut up.

CHAPTER FOUR

THE GOBLIN CHIEF

GORTOGH WAS NEVER meant to lead a goblin tribe. He lacked the strength to crush the skulls of his enemies. He could wield a blade, but never with enough power to best the other warriors of the tribe. By most measures of goblin worth, he was a weakling who should have died at the end of a sword long ago.

He was handsome by goblin standards, but that mattered little to goblin females. The handsomest goblin was usually the weakest warrior. And he was weaker than most. He had never found a mate. Strength and power made goblin females swoon, and he possessed neither.

But Gortogh was smarter than most of his kind. What he lacked in strength and dexterity he more than made up for in intelligence. Which is how he became the chief of his tribe. He had earned the title just like every goblin before him. By killing the previous chief in bloody combat.

With some help, of course.

Deep in the back of his cave, Gortogh faced Velanon

and tried to hold himself up and appear strong. He hated these visits from the elf. He feared the others in his tribe would learn of his deception if they caught him. They stood in absolute darkness. With both of them able to see clearly in the dark, there was no need for light. Gortogh crossed his arms and stared.

"I trust from your shiny new armor that everything went to plan?" the elf said.

Gortogh's hand fell absentmindedly to the black leather armor he now wore on his breast.

"Hogar is dead," he said. "I am chief now."

"The ring worked just as I told you it would."

Gortogh said nothing.

He preferred to think that he would have won the fight just as easily without the wicked ring the wizard had given him, but he knew in his heart it was a lie. In the heat of battle, at his urging, the ring had released a silent, unseen wave against the previous chief, weakening and slowing him. His once mighty swings had no strength behind them and became easy to dodge. His legs moved as though mired in mud. Gortogh had taken his head in a single stroke not long after.

"You've come to take the ring back?" Gortogh asked.

"No, no," the elf said. "You keep it. You might need it soon enough. No, in fact I am here to offer you something else. Something more powerful. Have you done what I asked?"

Gortogh's eyes opened wide at the mention of more power, but he quickly hid his surprise.

"I have sent out goblins to scout and to call to the

other tribes, but it will do no good. We are a large tribe, but they will not come to my call."

"They will come. It is the will of Ogrosh."

Gortogh hoped the elf could not see him roll his eyes in the darkness. He pondered a moment before addressing him again.

"Why are you doing this?"

"For the same reason I brought you the ring in the first place. I need a goblin's help, and you are the smartest I have found. Which is still not saying much."

Gortogh narrowed his eyes and flexed what muscles he had. Puny elf. He toyed briefly with the idea of using the elf's own ring against him and killing him, but he suspected it would do no good. He clenched his fists a few times and stared the elf down.

"Be careful, goblin. You would be wise to keep your brutish anger in check, or our future meetings will not be as pleasant."

The goblin chief took a deep breath and relaxed his fingers.

"That's better. I have had another vision, given to me by Ogrosh. A vision about you. He wishes you to unite the tribes in a single kingdom. Ogrosh wants you to be champion of all the goblin tribes."

This time, Gortogh could not hide his surprise.

"What does this mean? Ogrosh wishes me to be the leader of all goblins? How?"

It was all an act.

But a convincing one. Gortogh was smarter than even Velanon gave him credit for. The wizard had used the same tactic when they first met. He claimed to have had a vision from Ogrosh, the Blood God, god of all goblins. He said the ring was a gift from Ogrosh for him to destroy Hogar in battle and become chief of his tribe.

It's all lies, of course.

He knew the skill the wizard possessed. He knew the ring was only an item of magic and not something given divine power by Ogrosh. But Gortogh didn't care. The elf was offering him more than his grandest dreams, and he was going to take it.

"Ogrosh has given me an amulet of great power. One that will give you power over all of your kind. You will be Ogrosh's champion, and they will bow to you."

"And if they don't?"

"The power of the amulet is strong. It is blessed by Ogrosh himself. But you will still need strength in battle. For that, Ogrosh has granted you a great weapon. A sword of immense power for you to smite his enemies and to enforce his will upon his children. He chose you for this, Gortogh. You are his champion."

Velanon pulled from his pack a simple, bronze amulet that was engraved on both sides with symbols and writing Gortogh did not recognize. He did recognize the symbol in the center though. A fist with a single drop of blood falling from it. The symbol of Ogrosh.

The elf dangled the amulet in the air in front of him, and he took a step forward and grasped it. The wizard paused and let him stare at it a moment before reaching back into his pack and pulling out a longsword held in its scabbard. This, too, he handed to Gortogh.

Gortogh stared at it.

It was also covered in markings and symbols Gortogh didn't recognize. But in the sword, he could feel the hum of power. It tingled in his hands.

It was a much bigger weapon than most goblins wielded, but it still felt light in his hand. He let the amulet drop to the ground as he gripped the hilt in one hand and the scabbard in the other. With a light tug, Gortogh pulled the blade free from its leather prison and held it aloft. Even in pure darkness the blade seemed to shine.

Velanon punched him hard in the face.

Gortogh fell backward, stunned, and nearly took his own head off with his new toy. He tried to jump back up, but the elf's black boot was pressing down on his chest in an instant. The wizard held the amulet dangling over his face.

"You are a stupid goblin," he said. "The sword is *nothing*. It is a toy for boys to chop at each other with. This amulet is the *true* power of Ogrosh. *Never* let this out of your sight. Put it around your neck and do not take it off!"

The elf crushed his boot down harder, making it difficult for Gortogh to breathe. His hand quietly searched the ground for his dropped sword, as he thought to skewer the wizard right there.

"Do not make me kill you, goblin. Ogrosh's blessings will find another champion should you die this day."

With no further ceremony, Velanon dropped the amulet onto his chest and then stepped off. Gortogh scrambled back and quickly to his feet. He glanced to the side to see the sword lying in the dirt and then turned back to face the elf. He pulled the leather cord over his head and let the amulet fall unceremoniously to his chest.

Nothing.

No great power surged within him. No great strength filled his body. He picked it up and stared at it for another few seconds before pulling his shirt and leather armor away from his body and dropping the amulet beneath them.

"No!" the elf yelled. "Wear it where all can see it! They will know your power. They will know you are Ogrosh's champion."

Gortogh pulled the amulet back out and let it fall to his chest. With a nervous glance to his sword, he took a few steps and picked it up. He found the scabbard a few feet away and grabbed it as well. He tried to buckle the belt around his waist, but the sword was longer than his legs and it stuck awkwardly into the ground. After adjusting it a few times he finally gave up and draped the belt over his neck and shoulder with the longsword across his back.

"The amulet is the true power of Ogrosh, but the sword will serve you well in battle. It has a great power beyond its appearance. It will grant you immense strength in combat when you wield it. And at a thought, it can discharge a bolt of lightning. The lightning can be shot from the tip of the sword, or it can course down the blade and into your enemies. But the power is not without limits."

Gortogh drew the sword and stared at the blade in awe.

"How often can I use it?"

"The strength will last a while, maybe hours each day. The lightning, a few times per day at most. The magic of the blade will replenish itself, but you should still use it sparingly."

"Ogrosh has truly blessed me," Gortogh said.

It felt silly saying it, but there was no harm in letting the elf think he believed all this champion nonsense.

"Truly he has," the elf said. "And now Ogrosh wishes an offering from you. Something to show your faith."

Did the elf really believe this stuff? He can't. Gortogh backed away a step and eyed the wizard.

"You must build an army," Velanon said. "The smaller tribes will answer your call first. They will come to you, and you will become their chief."

"They have their own chief. They will not simply bow to me."

"They will. You will see. When they come and join with your tribe you will have many warriors under your command. But in order to gain the fealty of the bigger tribes you will need a show of force. Something to show the might and power of Ogrosh's champion."

"You want me to attack another tribe? That will only start a war among all the goblins."

"No. Ogrosh would not have you killing other goblins. They must join you. No, there is a village not far from your caves. Only a day's travel. It is small and ripe for the taking. I think you should attack there. Let your warriors spill the blood of the men and enjoy their women."

"I don't have enough warriors to attack a village!"

"More will come," Velanon said. "They will join Ogrosh's army with you as their general. You will see."

Gortogh heard shouting coming from the front of the cave. He stepped past Velanon to see what was going on and caught sight of some of his warriors yelling at him from outside. He turned back to say something else to the elf, but he was gone.

The goblin chief walked out of his cave, formerly Hogar's cave, and met his warriors.

"What going on?" Gortogh said, his speech suddenly sounding broken. He always spoke the way other goblins did when talking to them. It would not do him good for them to think he was smarter than them.

"Scouts come back," one of the warriors said. "Some bloody, some dead."

Gortogh looked past them at the scouts as they hobbled back into camp. The four that had the strength to walk on their own were carrying several others. A couple cried out in pain as the walking jostled them while others made no move at all. He wondered if they were dead or just unconscious from the pain. He could see arrows sticking out of the wounded.

If only Gortogh had a shaman in his tribe. The magic of the Blood God could heal them all. Perhaps one would come with one of the smaller tribes. If they same that is. The elf is probably just crazy.

More shouts came across the camp from the other side as two other goblins came running up to him.

"What now?" Gortogh said.

"Chiefs coming," one of them said. "Other chiefs coming just like you ask. Smaller tribes."

Gortogh looked back over his shoulder into the cave behind him and couldn't suppress a smile. Maybe he's not so crazy. Gortogh pulled his shoulders back and took a deep breath to puff his chest out a little more. He yanked his sword free and held it high for all of his warriors to see, but he had to fight the urge to shoot a bolt of lightning into the air. That was one trick he would save for later. The sunlight glinted off the bright blade, and Gortogh felt power surge through his muscles.

"Tell chiefs to come meet Ogrosh's champion!"

CHAPTER FIVE

A GOBLIN IN THE YARD

ELODY AND RINN walked silently in step the whole way home. When they reached the northern edge of the village and the road to their farm, Rinn stopped.

"I need to go into town," he said. "Dad wanted me to get the axe sharpened."

"Can I come?" Elody asked.

"Sure. I gotta run and grab the axe though. Meet you there."

He jogged off down the path and saw Elody head down the road into the village. He quickly trotted around the back of the house to where he'd left the axe in the stump and pulled it out in a quick motion. He glanced around the yard for his father but didn't see him, so he kept moving around the other side of the house toward the village. The path from their farm dropped him onto the main road through town, and he was in the square a minute later.

Rinn didn't see Elody anywhere, but he did spot someone who interested him. As he moved alongside a building, he leaned the axe against the wall and left it there as he crept off around the other side. Sneaking quietly along the wall, he slid up behind the girl who was standing next to a cart with her back to him.

"You're even more beautiful than the last time I saw you, Fawn Kerris" he whispered.

She jumped as he put his hand on her side. A little smile appeared on her lips, but she made no other move and did not turn to acknowledge him.

"How about since the last time you saw Leena?" she said, her smile turning to a scowl.

His eyes went wide and his body tensed, but he hid the reaction just as quickly and hoped she hadn't noticed.

"That cow?" Rinn said. "When would I have seen her? Her father only lets her out of the barn to graze."

He smiled and poked her gently in the back and was relieved to see that little smile creep back onto her face.

"That cow is my friend," she said, but she didn't stop smiling.

"Then perhaps you should walk her in the meadows more often."

She turned and smacked him on the arm.

"You're awful, Rinn!"

With her facing him, he took the opportunity to pull her back between the buildings and closer to him. She struggled against his grip, but only a little. She started to protest with a playful grin, but he cut her off as he pressed his lips to hers. They kissed for several seconds before she pulled away and smiled. When he leaned in again, she put her hand out and pushed him back.

"Rinn! Someone will see us."

"Let them see."

He pulled her in and kissed her again, but she broke it off more quickly this time and pulled back. Fawn glanced around nervously but then smiled back at him.

"You're terrible," she said. "My father would kill us both if he caught us."

Rinn snorted.

"Your father would have to catch me first."

He grinned and winked, and she gently pushed him in the chest again.

"Are you going to the party?" he asked.

"Of course. Everyone is going."

"Save a dance for me?"

"You know I can't dance with you," she said with a little smile.

"And why not?"

She looked down and kicked the dirt, her smile disappearing.

"You know why."

Rinn pushed her back as he turned and walked off.

"To the abyss with this town!"

"Rinn!"

She ran and caught up to him, but he threw her hand off and kept walking.

"I'm sorry, Rinn, I—"

"*I'm* the one who should be sorry! Sorry I never left this damn town!"

He turned back so abruptly that she almost ran into him.

"You know, everyone wants to hate me and blame me, but I can't control a damn dragon!"

"They don't hate—"

"The whole damn town can burn to the ground for all I care, and you with it!"

"Rinn, stop!"

He turned and walked away without stopping. She called after him again, and he could hear the tears in her voice, but he didn't turn back. He grabbed his axe as he came around the side of the building and went straight to the smithy across the street. Fawn was standing back by her cart, and he could see her looking at him, but he would not meet her gaze. She dropped her face into her hands, but he didn't look up. He walked into the smithy and dropped the axe next to the anvil where the smith was sitting.

"I need this sharpened, Warren."

The smith looked up from where he was hammering a horseshoe.

"You can wait 'til I'm done with this," he said.

Rinn glared at him, but the old man had already gone back to his work. Rinn finally looked away and then slumped down onto a stump a few feet away. He dropped his head into his hands and sat silently listening to the rhythmic clanging of Warren's hammer.

Damn this town.

He was still angry at Fawn, but he knew deep down that it was not her fault. He dropped his head between his knees and sat there thinking for a while. When he finally lifted his head, Warren looked up briefly to meet his eyes and then dipped the horseshoe into the bucket of water at his feet, sending steam into the air with a loud hiss. Rinn watched him work for another minute and then took a deep breath and sat up with his hands on his knees.

"If you wanna just leave that here, I'll bring it back to the farm when I'm done with it," Warren said. "Or you can sit there as long as you like."

He looked out into the square and then back to the smith.

"Thanks, Warren."

Rinn sat there a few more minutes and breathed slowly, taking in the heat and moisture in the air. When he had finally calmed down, he stood and walked back out into the square. He looked around for Elody again and made a particular point not to look in Fawn's direction. He could see her still watching him, but he wouldn't meet her gaze. As he scanned around, his eyes locked onto the back of a man he did not recognize standing stiffly in the square.

Rinn took a slow step toward the man, who was not looking in his direction. When he saw him turn at last to look down the street, Rinn recognized him.

"Berym?"

The knight turned and smiled.

"Good day, Rinn."

"I didn't recognize you without your armor."

"No need for armor on a nice day in a quiet village, but my sword is never far from me should I need it."

The knight patted his left side, and Rinn saw his

sword hanging from his belt. A woman turned at their conversation and offered a slight smile when she recognized Rinn.

"Rinn."

"Good morning, Mara."

"How's Malcom?" she asked. "I mean your father."

"He's well. I'll tell him you asked."

Rinn looked away, and Mara looked down awkwardly. Berym looked back and forth at them as a long pause hung in the air.

"A fine day," Berym said loudly. "Lots of work to be done."

Mara smiled and looked up at Rinn.

"Sir Berym has been helping me out the past few days. He's been chopping wood and helping fix a few things around the house. Getting ready for the first cold."

The knight smiled.

"It's just Berym."

"Oh, yes. I'm sorry I keep doing that. I've been lucky to have his help. It's been so long since I had a strong man around."

"I am happy to be of service, Lady Mara, but you are definitely in no need of a strong man. I dare say I don't know a man strong enough to handle you."

Rinn saw Mara blush. The knight turned back to look at him and gave him a little wink that made him smile as well.

"I must get back to the farm," she said as she turned.

"Here," Berym said, "let me carry that basket back. I

shall catch up with you shortly."

Mara smiled and handed over the basket she was carrying before walking off down the main road. Rinn and Berym watched after her as she left.

"A fine woman," the knight said. "Very lonely. As strong as any I've met, but lonely."

"She lost her husband and son," Rinn said.

"Aye, in the wars. She told me briefly of it when I offered to help her around the farm. I think we've both been happy for the company."

"Is it lonely being a knight?"

The knight turned to look at him.

"Sometimes," he said. "Most knights travel alone unless they are training a squire. Some travel together with the knight who trained them."

"Do you travel alone?"

"Mostly."

"Where is the knight who trained you?"

Berym looked down, and his hand fell to the hilt of his sword.

"Dead. Killed in the Kingdom Wars as well. Many good men died in that war."

"Did you fight in the war?"

"Some. I was still very young, even younger than you. I had only just received my shield. I was thrust into battle by my king when many of the knights of my kingdom were killed and he had no one left to throw at our neighbors."

"You fought for King Hallex, right?"

"Yes."

"I saw his symbol on your armor."

"I haven't the gold to buy new armor, but I do not wear the crest of my former king with any pride. In truth, I rarely wear the breastplate at all. He was a brutal man, and I would burn him from my chest and my soul if I could."

"Why did you fight for him if he was so bad?"

Berym locked eyes with him.

"Because he was my king. And I was a stupid boy who knew no better."

Rinn looked away from his gaze, not knowing what else to say. The knight looked up the street and then to the basket at his feet.

"I have never been in a real fight," Rinn said.

"Not even with the goblin attacks out here?"

"We haven't had more than a few skirmishes since I've been old enough, so I've never fought. I fought with boys when I was younger, and I've witnessed a few, but I've never fought myself."

"If you are lucky, you will never have to."

The knight smiled at him once more and turned to leave.

"Why don't you let people call you Sir Berym? That's your title isn't it?"

"It is a title that commands respect for no other reason than a king gave it to me. I will earn respect for my deeds, not my name."

"And you haven't earned it with your deeds?"

He paused and looked back.

"Not yet."

Berym picked up the basket and walked off down the road after Mara. Elody popped out of the stables a moment later and wandered over to Rinn who was still staring after the knight.

"Who was that?" she asked.

"Berym."

"He looks smaller without his armor."

Rinn laughed a little, and Elody started laughing too. She was still laughing and looking up the street after the knight when Rinn saw a woman come out of the shop and then quickly shuffle something behind her back when she saw them there.

"Oh, Elody!"

"Hello, Arina," Elody turned and said with a smile.

Rinn watched as the woman uncomfortably tried to keep whatever she was hiding behind her back while still appearing polite. He looked at Elody, but she seemed oblivious to it all.

"How are you?" Elody asked.

"Wonderful. Your dad told us all about your dragon. A boy, named Jalthrax, right?"

"Yes! He's amazing! I can't wait for the whole village to meet him!"

"Well, we can't wait either. We've never had a real dragonmage to call our own before."

Rinn noticed Elody start to say something, but then she looked up at him for a second and just smiled. Arina looked to Rinn and then looked down.

"Well, " she said, "I've got to be off. Getting things ready for the, uh, for dinner tonight. I've got to get dinner ready."

She turned down the road and pulled her hands quickly in front of her.

"Bye, Arina!" Elody yelled.

Rinn smiled at her and turned up the road back toward the farm. Elody fell into step behind him, and they walked the few minutes back in silence. As they neared the house, they saw their father striding purposefully toward them with a bow in his hand.

"Get in the house," he said. "Now."

"What's going on, Dad?" Rinn asked.

"Goblins."

***

Rinn stepped quietly down the front step. He snuck around the outside of the house and closer to the chicken coop. He was close enough now that he could see the goblin in all its ugliness.

Its skin looked green and rough and yet slimy at the same time. Its only clothing was a ratty strip of cloth that hung from a rope belt tied around its waist. In its stubby hand was a short sword. The grin on its ugly face said it was ready to use it.

Rinn drew his dagger and took a few deep breaths to try and prepare himself. He counted silently to three. He rounded the corner of the house and snuck along the side, trying to get closer.

The goblin was moving slowly toward the chicken coop with a leering smile. It got close to the fence, and the chickens jumped and fluttered in a big commotion. The goblin jumped back in surprise and caught sight of

76

Rinn. Both of their eyes went wide as they met. With a yell, Rinn leapt from hiding and charged.

The goblin gave a squeal of surprise, but it didn't move to retreat. Rinn yelled loudly, but it didn't seem afraid at all. He could see it grin and lick its lips as he charged in. It was ready for him.

He paused in his charge for a split second when he saw the smile on the creature's face, and it probably saved his life. While Rinn was looking at the goblin's eyes, its sword had come forward and was just hanging there in the air, waiting for him to spear himself on it.

The goblin flashed a look of annoyance and charged in with a yelp. It stabbed with its short sword, a killing shot straight for Rinn's gut. Rinn may not have been tested in actual combat, but he had been trained. By his father and the other men of the village. Most of them veterans of the war.

It won't be that easy.

Rin jumped back out of its reach and slapped the sword aside with his dagger. It overextended its reach trying for a quick kill, and Rinn drove his dagger back in trying for the same. The goblin skipped back and to the side, but Rinn still managed to cut it across its middle. It yelped in pain, and Rinn couldn't hide the smile on his face.

The goblin growled and slashed back with its sword. Rinn got his dagger up to parry it, but he wasn't used to fighting in close combat, or with someone who was swinging with force for a kill. His arm tingled from the strength of the blow, and he only just managed to hold onto his dagger. His smile turned to a grimace. Now it was the goblin's turn to smile.

It stabbed in again, and Rinn dodged to the side, but the goblin had calculated his move and slashed to the side where he had jumped. Rinn swung his dagger down quickly, just managing to deflect the sword, but he lost his grip. His dagger fell from his grasp.

Rinn knew in that instant that he would die. In the split second before the goblin's blade stabbed in, he thought of his little sister. Elody. *What will she do without me?*

The last thing Rinn saw as the goblin whooped and stabbed with its sword was a brilliant white light. The sound of the world around him went silent, replaced by ringing in his ears. He felt the ground slam hard against his back. He could still feel his body as he waited for death to take him. Then he heard Elody's voice. She sounded distant and faded.

"Rinn!"

It sounded like she was shouting at him underwater. Even through the fogginess he could hear the panic in her voice.

"Rinn, get up!"

Rinn tried to open his eyes. The world was blurry, but he could see. The ringing in his ears was dying down, and he could hear the sounds of the world returning.

"Rinn, it's getting up! Hurry!"

Rinn bolted upright.

It took a moment to remember he was on the ground. Things weren't making sense. As his vision cleared, he saw clearly the goblin laying on the ground in front of him. It was moving slowly, and it looked as dazed as he felt. Elody shouted from somewhere behind him.

"Rinn! To your right!"

He looked right and reached out. His hand closed over the hilt of his dagger lying in the grass. The fog in his head cleared in an instant. He grabbed the dagger and leapt forward. The goblin was flailing its arms and slapping them at the ground trying to get up.

Then Rinn was on top of it.

The goblin swung its arms and hit him a few times before he grabbed his dagger with both hands and plunged it into its chest. The goblin screamed and squealed loudly and tried to grab at the dagger, but its strength was quickly leaving. With one last punch at Rinn's face that only glanced off of his cheek, the goblin fell dead.

Rinn took a deep breath and stayed kneeling on the goblin until he heard Elody run up behind him. He had a sudden thought and picked his head up to scan the yard, but he saw no more goblins.

"I'm sorry, Rinn. I thought he was going to kill you."

"He was. Good thing he didn't know I have my little sister here to protect me."

"I would have shouted to close your eyes, but I didn't know if it would understand me and do it too."

"I'm okay. Just stunned for a second."

As he stood up, she threw her arms around him and grabbed him in a great hug. He could feel the tears rolling down her cheek as hers pressed against his. He hugged her so tight that he thought he would squeeze the life from her, but he wouldn't let go. They held each other like that for several seconds. He felt her arms slacken, and she moved her head to look over his shoulder.

"Dad!" she yelled.

Rinn turned to see the group of men coming out of the woods. Elody had pulled away and was already running out to meet them. Berym was leading the group, and he saw the other four men walking behind him. Two of the men carried a third between them.

Dad?

The front of the man's shirt was drenched in blood.

Chapter Six

The War Party Returns

ELODY BREATHED AS soon as she saw her father's face. He wasn't the one the men were carrying, he was walking behind them. Elody ran to meet him, but he pushed past her with only a quick look.

"Rinn, go and fetch the village elders," her father said.

Rinn looked confused. Elody saw that the man between the others was Gald. He was bleeding and crying out in pain. Her father looked at the goblin lying dead on the ground and then back to them.

"The elders, Rinn," her father said.

Rinn nodded dumbly and turned to leave.

"Rinn," her father said.

He turned back to face their father who was pulling the dagger from the dead goblin's chest.

"Take this, son."

Rinn could only nod again as he took the dagger and ran off toward the village.

"Elody, get in the house."

"No, Daddy. Tell me what is happening."

"You're a young girl and this doesn't concern you."

"That goblin could have killed us both if we hadn't fought and killed it!"

Her father looked her over and then looked at the dead goblin.

"You fought with your brother?"

"I'm a dragonmage," she said defiantly.

She tried to sound brave and strong, but it came out sounding a bit too much like a child trying to prove she is a grown up. Her father looked down his black mustache at her with the same look he always had. Elody crossed her arms and stared him down. He nodded and turned back to face the other men without a word.

"Put him down there."

The men holding Gald lowered him gently to the ground, but he still cried out in pain. Elody hadn't noticed Berym before, but he was there now. He knelt down in front of Gald and ripped open the man's shirt. Elody saw a large gash opened up across his side with blood pouring out of it.

"We need to stop the bleeding, Malcom," Berym said to her father.

Elody watched silently as the men tried to stop the flow of blood. His shirt and trousers were getting completely soaked. She stared at the scene in front of her and everything seemed to slow. She didn't know how long she watched before she realized her father was talking to her.

"Elody."

She pulled her gaze away and looked at him.

"Go in the house and fetch some bandages."

She nodded and ran into the house. She dug around in a pile of clothes before finally settling on an old shirt of Rinn's. She pulled it up from the pile and hurried back outside, handing it to her father.

He grabbed the shirt from her with a nod and took a small dagger off of his belt. He made small cuts in the fabric and then tore it into long strips. Elody noticed that the other men resting on the ground were also hurt. Blood stained their clothing everywhere she could see.

Her father handed the strips to Berym as he tore them off. The knight was trying to stop Gald's bleeding, but it didn't seem to Elody to be helping much. He wrapped long strips around his back and pulled them tight, causing Gald to cry out in pain, and then tied them off.

Her father handed her a handful of bandages and then set to work on one of the men. Elody went to another and knelt down to examine the wounds on his leg. It didn't look deep, and he didn't seem to be in much discomfort. She started to slide the strip under his leg when he grabbed her hand.

"Tend to your father, girl. I can bandage my own leg."

She looked confused and turned to look at her dad who was helping the other man. She saw a blood stain on her father's sleeve. It was big. Elody walked toward him slowly, looking at his arm. It looked like a lot of blood.

She took a bandage from the pile on the ground and scooted over to her father. She slowly touched his arm and pulled it toward her. He lifted his head and locked eyes with her as she bent her head down and started tying off his wound. She couldn't hold his gaze.

Don't cry. Don't let him see you cry.

When she finished her work, he stood and pulled her chin up to look at him. She tried to hold it in, but as she raised her eyes to meet her father's, it all came pouring out. He grabbed her and pulled her to him in a tight hug. She buried her face in his blood-stained shirt and cried.

"It's okay," he whispered. "I'm all right. It's just a little cut."

He kept repeating himself in a soft voice, trying to stop the tears. The other men looked up as they heard voices coming from around the house. Rinn was returning with what sounded like the whole village. Her father gave her one last squeeze and then pulled back and squared her shoulders.

"Stand up tall, Elody. Be strong."

She nodded feebly and wiped her eyes on her shoulder. Rinn came around the house with a dozen other townspeople in tow. All of them stopped as one when they saw the goblin corpse lying on the ground. A few turned their heads to look at her father and the other men.

Berym had Gald wrapped completely around his midsection. The bandages were not as soaked with blood as the rest of his clothes, and it looked to Elody like they might have stopped the bleeding. Berym whispered something to the other men and then stood.

"He might make it," Berym said. "It doesn't look good, but if we can keep him alive through the night he might have a chance. We should see if we can call for a priest from Buxbaum though."

All of the villagers held onto each other for support and watched silently as the men continued to press against his wounds. A few turned back to her father.

"What happened, Malcom?" one of the elders, Laren, finally asked.

"We killed four goblins up near the ridge," her father said. "They came around some rocks and caught us by surprise. Once we started fighting, one of 'em ran off into the woods. He must've made it back here before we did. Rinn and Elody killed him where he lays."

The villagers looked at the goblin again and then looked back and forth at Rinn and Elody.

"We fought hard," her father said. "Berym killed two of 'em himself. Gald killed another one before the last one tore him open."

They all turned to look at Gald who was unconscious and breathing slowly. They watched for several seconds before turning back. Mara looked to Malcom.

"Are there more out there?" she asked.

"We saw none in the forest or up near the mountains, but there are lots of caves up there, and there could be some hiding where these five came from. We didn't try to go after anymore."

"What are we going to do?" asked Arina as she turned to Laren beside her.

"We set a watch, to start," he replied.

"Can we get Elody's dragon early?" Warren asked.

All eyes turned to look at Elody. She looked back at them all and shook her head.

"I don't think so."

"Why not?" he asked. "We paid for the damn dragon so it would protect the village!"

Elody looked at the ground and unconsciously stepped a little behind her father.

"I'm sorry," she said. "It's just not done that way."

Berym stepped up to stand beside Malcom.

"We will burn torches at the edge of the village and post a watch. The torches must burn all night, and the watch must be all day and night. I can guard through the night, but someone else will need to stand during the day."

"What of the outlying farms?" asked Laren. "Malcom's farm, and many others, are too far out of the village square to post a watch everywhere."

"Don't you worry about my farm, Laren," her father said. "Not your responsibility to protect my family."

He pointed down to the goblin lying dead.

"We'll take care of ourselves."

"Nice that you got a dragonmage protecting your farm," Laren said, "but what about the rest of us? What're we supposed to do?"

"I will patrol the outer farms," Berym said stepping forward. "We should have enough warning if anything comes."

Everyone nodded in unison.

"Go back to your homes now," Malcom said. "There's

nothing more to be done here."

"Who will take Gald?" Arina asked.

"I will tend him," Mara said, "with Berym's help."

Berym nodded to Mara and then nodded to the other men to pick him up gently and follow them. The rest turned and hurried back to the village. Back to their homes to see to their own protection and families. Rinn and Elody both moved beside their father. She waited until they were all out of earshot.

"I'm sorry, Daddy."

"Nothin' to be sorry about," he said.

He turned around and put his arm around both of them.

"Let's get back up to the house."

CHAPTER SEVEN

A LATE NIGHT AFFAIR

RINN QUIETLY PULLED the door closed behind him as he snuck out of the house. He paused and leaned in to listen for any sound from inside. After a few seconds of silence he stepped away from the door and then walked off down the path toward town.

He could see the firelight from the torches all around the square, and he could see many more posted around the distant farms. Rinn was used to the village being completely dark for his late night wanderings, and he found that though he could see better with the light, he couldn't hide nearly as well.

He walked quietly into town until he reached the first house and then he started sneaking carefully between the buildings. The torches gave off an eerie, orange glow all around the square, but it also made for many shadows along the walls. He used these deep shadows to his advantage and stayed well out of the light.

Rinn crept down several alleyways until he reached his destination. There, he stood silently in the shadows and waited. Minutes passed. He practiced holding perfectly still while staying hidden and waited.

After several minutes of standing, unmoving, he heard footsteps. They were hurried but light, and he could tell by the sound it was who he was waiting for.

Fawn.

Her face shown dimly in the torchlight of the square as he watched her search the shadows. She can't see me. He smiled to himself as she became more worried with each passing second.

"Here," he said quietly.

Rinn stepped out of the shadows just enough for her to see him and then disappeared back between the buildings. She looked relieved as she hurried over and slid in next to him.

"I got your note," she said.

"I see that."

"We shouldn't be out here tonight, Rinn."

"I needed to see you."

"Gald almost died today. He might still die."

"I know. I was there."

"There could be goblins out here!"

"There aren't any goblins. And if there are, I'm here to protect you."

"You're going to get us both in trouble or killed."

"I had to see you. I wanted to apologize for… for the way I acted. I didn't mean to get so mad, and I didn't mean to yell at you."

"It's not your fault."

"It is. I got angry, but it wasn't at you. I had to see you

tonight, goblins be damned!"

She scrunched her face, but the little smile on his lips soon had her smiling as well. She gave him a playful slap on the arm, and he smiled even bigger. She tried to slap him again, her smile growing wider, but he grabbed her hand mid-swing and pulled her to him. He bent down and kissed her firmly on the lips before she could open them to protest.

Their lips stayed locked in a kiss for what felt like forever before he finally pulled his head back slowly. Rinn's eyes were closed, and he blew a quiet whistle as he pulled away. When he opened them, she was smiling back at him and swaying her head with a slight blush.

"Will you dance with me at the party?" he asked.

"They haven't even decided if there will be a party. I heard my dad saying that the elders really didn't want to cancel it tonight, but it felt wrong after Gald. He said they might still have it tomorrow."

"Well, if they have it, will you dance with me?"

She stopped her swaying and looked down.

"Why do you keep asking when you already know the answer?"

"Because I want to dance with you!"

She shushed him and looked around hurriedly to see if anyone had heard him before speaking again.

"And you know that I can't," she said.

"It's only a dance. It doesn't have to mean anything more than that."

"My father said that you killed a goblin in the raid. Is that true?"

"It wasn't a raid, but I killed a goblin that came onto our farm, yes."

"He sounded impressed talking about you."

She smiled as she said it, but Rinn's face turned hard in the torchlight.

"Of course he did! It's impressive when worthless old Rinn can manage to kill himself a goblin!"

"He didn't mean it like that."

"Sure he didn't."

They stood silently, awkwardly, neither one looking up at the other.

"I just want a dance," he said finally.

She put her hand to his cheek and lifted his head.

"Maybe I can save one for you."

His eyes shined in the torchlight as a little smile found its way to his face.

"Maybe," she said with a gleam in her eye.

He smiled and wrapped his arms around her in a big hug. She started laughing, and he picked her up off the ground and spun her around, which only made her laugh harder.

"Shhh! Stop! You're going to wake everyone and scare them half to death!"

He put her down with a big smile. From somewhere behind her he heard footsteps on the road. He pushed her behind him and stepped back deeper into the shadows.

"Go," he whispered, "I'll see you tomorrow."

She turned behind him and hurried down the alleyway and into the night. Rinn leaned back into the shadows and listened to the footsteps that approached. He knew in a moment who it was. He could hear the soft ring of metal as Berym's mail armor swayed with his steps.

Rinn waited for him to pass.

Berym glanced down the alley between the buildings but quickly moved on, not seeing him at all. Rinn smiled and moved behind Berym to follow his footsteps through the town. He followed for several steps, the knight never noticing he was there, before he decided that it was best not to play tricks tonight.

He fell back a bit and then stepped out into the torchlight in the square and made an effort to make his steps louder. Berym spun around and tugged at his sword, but seeing Rinn, he let the hilt fall back to his side.

"Rinn?"

"It's me."

"What are you doing out tonight? I could have taken your head off."

"Only if you heard me," he said and smiled.

Berym didn't smile back, but he walked closer to stand in front of him.

"Odd night to take a stroll around town," the knight said.

"I couldn't sleep. Thought you might like some company on patrol."

"And I suppose you wore lavender for me as well?"

He crossed his arms over his chest and wore a big grin on his face. Rinn grabbed his shirt and brought it up to his nose. The knight was right, it smelled of sweet lavender.

Like Fawn.

Rinn looked up with a shrug and a sly smile, and the knight burst out laughing. A loud, belly laugh that made Rinn look around to see if anyone was awakened by the commotion. It took Berym a few breaths to stop laughing, but the smile never left his face.

"Well, come on then," he said. "Since you're already out on official business, I welcome the company."

He waved his arm as he walked down the road. Rinn hurried a few steps to catch up and then fell in step beside him. They strolled along for several minutes in silence as Rinn followed, not knowing where they were headed.

"How long will you be out here?" Rinn asked.

"All night."

"No one will relieve you?"

"No one needs to. I'll sleep through the morning once the sun rises."

Rinn nodded and kept up his pace. They walked past the last home in town and then along the path to one of the outer farms. The Kerris farm. Rinn suddenly worried about Fawn and whether she made it home safely.

"This is your girl, yes?"

Rinn looked up at him and then back to the house.

"One of them," he said blithely.

"A man doesn't need more than one good woman."

"You sound like my dad."

"Smart man, your father."

They walked past the farmhouse, and Berym made a turn around the outside of the house and headed back down the path toward another farm.

"How did you know?" Rinn asked.

"About you and the Kerris girl? I see more than you know."

"You didn't see me hiding when you walked past."

"Didn't I?"

He smiled as Rinn turned to look at him.

"No, I don't think you did."

"You're right, I didn't."

They both laughed.

Rinn saw that they were coming up on his own farm. Hope Dad's still asleep. They walked around the outside and to the tree line and stopped. Berym peered out into the darkness through the trees and stood silently for several seconds. Then he turned and headed around the outside of the house and back into town. When they reached the square, he stopped in the middle of the torches and faced Rinn.

"That was your first kill today," Berym said.

"My first real fight."

"Was it what you imagined?"

"I don't know what I imagined. I was scared."

Rinn stared down at the ground.

"I still get scared before every battle," Berym said. "And I've been in more than enough for one man's lifetime."

"I would have died if my sister hadn't saved me."

"Then you're lucky she was there."

Rinn nodded.

"Tell me what happened," Berym said.

"The goblin came into the yard and was coming toward the house. I snuck out around the other side. He was almost to the house. I ran out and charged, trying to overpower him. He was fast. Faster than I thought he could be."

"Goblins are quick," Berym said. "Many a man has died thinking he could outrun a goblin or two."

"I held my own against him, but he knocked the dagger out of my hand, and I had nothing else to fight with. I remember thinking about Elody. That I would die, and she would be next. I didn't see any of it, but she cast a spell that stunned both of us. I couldn't see anything, but then I heard her. She was shouting at me, and I came out of it just before the goblin did and got to my dagger first."

"You definitely have your sister to thank for being alive then."

Rinn looked down again and nodded.

"There is no shame in someone saving your life," the knight said. "I owe mine to more people than you could know."

"She's my baby sister."

"Not anymore she's not. Accepting help is something we all have to do once in a while. Don't let pride get in the way of you becoming a man."

Rinn looked up and smiled a little.

"Why did you charge the goblin head on with nothing but a dagger? That was reckless and dangerous."

"I had to stop him before he got to the house."

"Yes, but why attack head on? It does not play to your strength."

"I can hold my own."

"Of course you can, but it's not your strength. Tell me, would you think me foolish for trying to use the shadows and sneak around in the darkness?"

Rinn looked him up and down. Even just standing there and swaying slightly as he talked, Rinn could hear the chain mail of the hauberk rattling as it hung to his knees. He doubted the knight could sneak through a busy blacksmith's shop.

"I don't think you'd be very good at hiding," Rinn said with a smile.

"Right you are. And you are no good at frontal combat with a dagger. Unless you have some skill I'm unaware of, you don't want to bring a dagger to a sword fight."

"Then I should have snuck up on him?"

"That thought didn't occur to you?"

"It did, but I was scared. I wasn't thinking very clearly."

"That will always be there. You can lessen that fear with training, but it never goes away. You can only try to ignore it. Learn to use the skills you are blessed with. They will serve you much better than trying to fight as someone you are not. That said, I can teach you some skill with a blade. It never hurts to learn another weapon."

He smiled at Rinn and slapped him on the shoulder.

"Get back home now. I'm pretty sure your father has no idea you're out here, and I doubt he would let you out of chores tomorrow morning even if he did."

Rinn started to walk off and then turned back.

"Thanks," he said.

"Thanks for the company," Berym said.

Rinn walked a few steps before the knight shouted at his back.

"In the future, I prefer rosewater!"

Rinn chuckled and shook his head. He could hear Berym's bellowing laugh following him all the way back to the farm.

***

Rinn crept up to the door and put his ear against it. No noise from inside. He reached for the pull and heard a sound from the darkness behind him that made him jump. His father cleared his throat.

"You really think that was smart?" his dad asked.

Rinn straightened up and turned to face him.

"I was chatting with Berym."

"That's not what I asked," his father said.

"Why do you make everything a question?"

"Because I don't want to give you all of the answers in life."

"I needed to see Fawn. That's where I went."

"Just Fawn?"

"Yes."

His father shook his head and sighed.

"What would you do with you if you were me?"

"I wouldn't ask so many questions."

"I'm serious, Rinn."

"I am too."

"What would you do?" his father asked.

"What do you want me to do?"

"You were already born by the time I was your age. Your mother was almost Elody's age."

"So, I should have children because you did?"

"No, Rinn, that's not what I'm saying. Just that... you need to think about what you want to do with your life."

"I'm doing what I want, and it's working just fine for me."

"Do you really believe that?"

No, but he wasn't about to tell him that.

"Look... I don't know what I would have done without you after your mother died. But I've kept you here long enough. Now that your sister has her dragon, she'll be making her own way soon. Maybe it's time you did the same."

"Are you telling me to leave?"

"How long do you think Fawn is going to wait around for you? There are other men in this village who'd love to have that girl."

"Maybe it's not up to me," Rinn said.

His father shook his head. When he looked back up, he was smiling.

"What's so funny?" Rinn asked.

"Your grandfather hated me," he said. "Did I ever tell you that? Didn't want me near his daughter. Said I was slow and stupid, and there was no way he'd let me drag his daughter down with me."

What?

Rinn had never heard this story. He couldn't believe his father was telling it now. Dad was a quiet man, but he and Rinn did have lots of talks. Just nothing that was very personal about the man's life. He loved stories about Rinn's mother though. So did Rinn.

"Your mother came from a good family. I was just a farmer with no land and no money. But I worked hard. That wasn't good enough for your grandfather though. Your mother was... well, let's just say she was destined for more than living out a quiet life on a farm with the likes of me."

"What happened? I mean, how did you get her?"

"You win a woman's heart, Rinn, and it doesn't matter much what her father has to say about it. I loved your mother like crazy, and she loved me just the same. So, we left. She took a little money she had, and I took a little money I had, and we left Havnor in the middle of the night."

Rinn couldn't believe what he was hearing. His mother was always so beautiful and proper. The idea of her sneaking off in the middle of the night with some dirty farmer, even if it was his dad, just sounded impossible to him.

There's a lot I don't know about Mom, I guess.

"Where did you go?" Rinn asked.

"Baglund at first. It was the closest city, and we were on foot. But I found work, and she found work, and we... we made it work."

"What did her father do?"

"Nothing. He came and found us, but he could see in her eyes that there was nothing he could do. I don't think I ever told you that story."

"No," Rinn said.

"Maybe I should have told it sooner. Your mother... she was spirited. Once she set her heart on something, there was no stopping her. I just needed to convince her that *I* was where her heart belonged."

His father walked over and put a hand on his shoulder.

"Just do the same," his father said.

"But how do I convince her?" Rinn asked.

His father laughed. Not a sound Rinn had heard a lot since his mother died. Almost nine years she'd been gone. She was always the happy one. He missed her laugh.

"If you can't figure out how to do that," his father said, "then you've got much bigger problems than I thought."

Rinn was beginning to see his father in a different way. Maybe he wasn't as hard as Rinn had always thought. His father turned him toward the door.

"Come on," he said. "You're not getting out of morning chores just because you stayed out all night galavanting."

Rinn chuckled.

Still Dad.

CHAPTER EIGHT

A CELEBRATION

ELODY SHIFTED UNCOMFORTABLY in her robes as she stood on the little platform the village had built. She felt like she was on display. In fact, she was. The whole village had turned out tonight for a party to celebrate her, and she felt self-conscious standing there in front of everyone.

Everyone was eating and laughing and having a good time as the sun set. A dance floor had been cleared in the village square, but before the music got playing, everyone wanted to come and congratulate her.

The little platform she now stood on was only a few inches off the ground, but it was placed at the far end of the party, and the area in front of it had been kept clear to allow a line of people. For the last hour since the party had started, one person after another had finished their meal and then walked over to offer words of congratulations.

Elody smiled through it all and thanked each of them for their well wishes and for helping her through her training. Her father stood just to her side and reminded her to thank them for helping her. As if anyone in the town will let me forget it.

"You did good, Elody," Warren said walking up. "Money well spent, you ask me. Can't wait to get a look at your little dragon. Probably scare the piss outta them goblins next time they come back!"

He laughed a hardy laugh, and her father laughed along with him. Elody could only smile and chuckle a little. Rinn snorted behind her.

"Thank you for all your help with my training," she said. "I couldn't have done it without you."

She had repeated almost those exact words so many times tonight that they'd lost all sincerity. She just kept smiling and shaking hands or hugging the ones who leaned in. She was glad the old smith offered his hand.

"Don't mention it," Warren said. "Money well spent,"

The old smith looked past her to Rinn and shook his head. He moved on to her father and offered a hand and a smile.

"Malcom," he said. "Beautiful girl you got there. We're all real proud of her."

"So am I, Warren."

"What's the word on Gald?"

"Mara sent for a healer first thing this morning. Hoping one can come by tomorrow, but he's alive for now. Berym says Mara's taking good care of him, and his breathing is easier."

"I'll have to stop in tomorrow and see him."

Malcom nodded as Warren walked past him and back

to the party.

"How long do I have to stand here?" Elody asked.

"Until everyone has had a chance to say hello," her father said.

"What about me?" Rinn said. "Do I have to be here?"

"Yes," Malcom said.

Elody heard him sigh behind her and turned around to see him sulking with his arms crossed.

"At least you're not the center of attention," she said.

"Oh, I am. Just not the good kind of attention."

"That's enough you two," her father said.

He stepped down from the platform and walked off to where the village men were all gathered in a circle. They looked to be in a tense discussion as they parted and made room for him to step in. Elody turned back to look at Rinn again and saw him suddenly straighten up and brush his hair to one side. She spun back around and saw three girls, her old friends, coming up together.

Fawn, Leena and Lilith were all wearing big smiles as they came up one at a time and gave her a hug. She smiled genuinely at them and stepped down off the platform to talk.

"Oh, El, we're all so proud of you," Leena said.

"We can't wait to meet Jalthrax," Lilith said.

"I can't wait to bring him home," Elody said.

She noticed Fawn looking past her to Rinn. Elody stared at her trying to catch her eye, and when she finally did, they both had the biggest smile.

"Oh, we're so excited to have you back home for good!" Lilith said. "We missed you when you were gone all those weeks!"

"What're you gonna do once you bring him home?" Leena asked. "Are you going to go looking for the goblins?"

"My daddy says the goblins are gone," Lilith said.

"That's not what my dad says," Fawn said as she joined in.

"We killed five of them," Rinn said from behind Elody. "That's about all the warriors a tribe would have. I doubt we'll see anymore for a long time."

"Plus we have a strong, handsome knight protecting us!" Leena said.

All the girls giggled, even Elody.

"Berym won't be here forever," Rinn said. "Then it'll be up to the strong, young men of the village to protect you girls."

"Strong men?" Fawn said. "Let me know when you see one."

The girls snickered.

"Strong enough for any one of you," Rinn said. "Maybe even two of you."

He crossed his arms with a sly grin.

Fawn's face tightened and turned red while the other girls smiled and blushed.

"We don't need your protection," Fawn said. "My dad says that's why we paid for Elody."

"No one paid for Elody!" Rinn said, his arms dropping to his side.

Fawn was stunned silent for a moment by the tone of his voice, but her own anger quickly returned.

"Well, that's why everyone paid so much money. So she could protect us. We still might find other uses for strong, young men though. We need someone to chop our wood."

The girls couldn't contain themselves and burst out laughing. But Elody didn't laugh. She hung her head and closed her eyes.

"Oh, we can't wait to have you back around, El!" Leena said.

She picked her head back up and smiled as they all waved and went back to join the rest of the village. She stepped up onto the platform and looked to the side for her father but forgot he wasn't there.

I'm alone.

Then, as if he sensed her needs, Rinn stepped onto the platform beside her and put his arm around her. He gave her a little squeeze before letting her go.

A few more of the villagers walked up to tell Elody how proud they were, and she smiled and thanked each of them. But as soon as they were out of sight, her chin would slump down to her chest. Across the square, the music had started up. People started dancing. She and Rinn both watched silently.

"Good evening, Lady Elody, Rinn."

They both turned and smiled when they saw Berym. The knight was wearing his chain armor, like always. But it looked like he had polished and cleaned it up. He twirled his hand and took a bow.

"Congratulations to you," Berym said. "There are not many who can achieve what you have. You should be very proud of yourself. Everyone else here seems to be."

He waved his hand out to the villagers who were all drinking and dancing and celebrating. It felt to Elody like she and Rinn were the only ones who weren't.

"I only hope that I don't let them all down," she said.

"I have faith you won't," Berym said.

They all turned and watched in silence as everyone danced.

"Is that lavender I smell?" Berym said, leaning in.

Rinn snickered.

"I don't smell anything," Elody said.

Berym stood back up and smiled.

"That Fawn sure is a lovely girl," he said, winking at Rinn. "Someone ought to go and dance with her."

He smiled and bowed before walking off to join the group of men who were still talking near the food. Rinn and Elody stood on the platform and watched the rest of the village dance. With the party in full swing, no one was coming over anymore.

Neither of them made a move to join in.

They watched together as one of the young men in the village, just a little older than Elody, walked over to Fawn. They couldn't hear him, but he extended his hand to her, and she smiled as she took it and followed him. Rinn stepped down off the platform and took a step toward them but then stopped just as suddenly. With a slump of his shoulders, he climbed back up next to his sister.

"I hate this town," he said.

"I know you do."

"I can't stand it here anymore."

"Then why stay?"

"I couldn't leave you and Dad."

"Haven't you heard? I'm the great protector of the village."

He turned to look at her. No one else was paying attention to the two of them standing there. The whole party went on around them and didn't seem to notice them at all. She watched all of her friends dancing with a wistful look.

"I wish I could dance with the boys," she said.

"Then go dance. It's your party. Any of them would love to dance with you."

"I don't know how. While all my friends were learning to sew and dance and cook, I was learning how to cast spells and kill goblins. I'm not a girl who gets to dance with boys."

"Don't let them decide who you are, El. You're the only one who decides your life for you. You don't owe them anything."

She looked into his eyes.

"Neither do you."

He looked down and sighed.

"I wish that were true."

"How is it any less true for you than it is for me?"

"Because I chose the training, and I let everyone down. You are their shining hero."

"I never asked to be."

They stood in silence watching everyone laugh and dance.

"Can I tell you a secret?" she said. "I was going to run away when you got married. When I was little, and you were in training, I made this plan that I was going to leave when you got married and could take care of Dad and the farm. Mom made me promise when she died that I would take care of the two of you, but I figured if you had a wife, she could take care of you. So I was gonna leave. Maybe move to Havnor."

"Why did you want to leave?"

"I don't know. I just didn't want to spend my whole life in this village. I used to beg Mom to take me to Havnor when she would visit Aunt Jelena. There was so much more to see there. So much more to do. I just didn't want to stay here. I wanted to see the world."

"You can still leave, El. They can't force you to stay."

Elody looked out at her friends and family. All the people she'd ever known in her life. She shook her head.

"I can't leave," she said. "Fawn was right. They paid for me. They didn't buy me, but they might as well have. I have a responsibility."

"Don't let them do that to you. You can do whatever you want."

"They would have done it to you too."

"But I asked for it. I begged Mom to let me train. I never planned to run away. I don't want to see the world. I planned to stay right here and get married and protect my family and my village."

They watched as another boy pulled Fawn onto the dance floor. Elody thought she saw her look their way and freeze for a second, but she just turned and kept dancing. Rinn hung his head.

"Now the only thing I want is to be gone from here," he said.

"You can. No one expects you to stay."

"You mean no one wants me to stay."

"I do. I'd be all alone if you left."

He put his arm around her and pulled her close. She laid her head on his chest and hugged him.

"Well, I'm not going anywhere right now," he said.

"But you will."

"Maybe after Dad's gone."

"Don't say things like that."

Rinn hugged her tighter.

"Hey," he said. "Thanks for saving my life yesterday."

"That's what us protectors do."

He laughed and pushed her away with a playful shove.

"I'm supposed to be your protector!" he said.

"Maybe we'll just have to protect each other."

He ruffled her hair and jumped down off the platform.

"I'm gonna go find something to drink."

"Are you going to ask Fawn to dance?"

He watched Fawn dance with a smile on his face and then turned back to look at her.

"No, I don't think so. Not tonight."

"Probably for the best. I think Berym's sweet on her."

Rinn laughed again as he walked off, leaving her standing on the platform all by herself. She watched as the boys slowly found their courage and started asking her friends to dance. For the first time that night she found herself wishing someone would walk over to her.

CHAPTER NINE

FETCH THE DRAGON

ELODY PULLED HER dress robes over her head and smoothed them against her body. She turned to stare at her reflection, and a little smile crept across her face. She gripped the sides of the black silk and swished her hands.

She couldn't resist doing a few twirls in front of the mirror and watching the robes float into the air and then settle back down against her small frame.

"I never liked the robes," Rinn said as he pushed the door open and walked into the room. "They were always a little too silky for me."

"You never even got to wear them."

"I stole one from the master's closet one day and tried it on. I caught a glimpse of myself in the mirror, and I looked like a girl."

She looked at him through the mirror and wrinkled her brow in annoyance.

"All new dragonmages wear the same robes," she said.

"Well, I guess I was destined to wear something else

then."

She ignored him and looked back at herself in the mirror.

"You look great," he said. "Mom would be proud."

Elody turned around and smiled at him.

"Are you ready?" he asked.

Elody looked back at the mirror. Was she ready? She had spent the last three years of her life training for today. She had spent the last two in the company of an egg while she slept. All of that had just been practice. She nodded to herself in the mirror.

"I'm ready," she said.

He smiled without a word, and it only got bigger as she turned back and looked at herself one more time in the mirror.

"Well, I'm ready when you are," he said.

She nodded again and headed for the door.

"Are you sure you don't want to check the mirror one more time?"

She smacked him on the arm, and he stepped out of the way to let her through the door. With a little laugh he fell into step behind her.

"Dad's waiting for you outside."

She hurried her step a little as she went out the door and made a sweep of the yard. He was there, standing near the road waiting for them. She walked across the yard with Rinn following behind her and stopped in front of her father.

"How do I look?" she asked.

"You look... powerful," he said.

He smiled, and Elody threw her arms around him and gave him a big hug.

"Are you coming with us?" she asked.

He shook his head.

"Some of the men and I are heading up to the ridge to do some scouting. Looking for more goblin sign."

She nodded and bit her lip. She didn't know what to say, so she gave him another hug.

"Be safe," she whispered

"I will, little girl."

She turned to see her brother standing a few feet away and waiting patiently. When she looked at him, he moved up beside her, and the two of them walked up the path toward the forest. Elody glanced back over her shoulder and saw her father already crossing the yard to get his bow from the side of the house.

"They haven't found anything in four days," she said. "Why do they keep going up to the ridge? There aren't anymore goblins up there."

"I guess just to make sure. Dad seemed confident that the ones we killed were the hunters of a small tribe and we won't see anymore trouble from them."

She looked back over her shoulder again, but they were already in the woods far enough that she couldn't see her father.

"I wish we could go out with him," she said.

"Me too. We killed a goblin. Maybe once you have your dragon he'll let us go with him. We look a lot scarier to a bunch of goblins bringing a dragon with us. Even if he is a scrawny one."

Elody bristled.

"He's not scrawny! He's bigger than most dragons his age."

"Can he breathe ice yet?"

"Only a little puff. But it might be enough to kill a goblin."

They both smiled.

"Maybe he can eat some," Rinn said. "Save us some of our food."

"Ugh! I don't want him eating goblins! He can already hunting for himself. He has been since the day he was born. I only bring food to strengthen the bond."

Rinn nodded as he kept watch all around them. Elody could see that he was tense, but she couldn't let go of how happy she felt. She was practically skipping. He smiled at her and shook his head.

They silently walked the hour to the cave just as they had done every day for the past week. Rinn kept a watchful eye on the woods around them, but there was no trouble. By the time they reached the bottom of the mountain, he could barely hide his disappointment. For the past few days, Rinn had always waited at the bottom of the mountain path, but this time he followed her up and waited outside the cave.

"When you come out of there this time, you'll be a full-fledged dragonmage," he said with a smile.

Elody thought she detected a note of pride in his voice. I hope it's pride.

She turned and took a deep breath before walking in. This would be her tenth, and most likely final, trip into this particular cave. She came first three years ago to ask for the gift of an egg from the Silver Queen. Then she came again nearly a year later when an egg was laid. Finally she came again after two more years when the egg was ready to hatch, and then every day for the past week.

When she left the cave this time, she would be a dragonmage. Elody realized that her pace had slowed. She took another breath, held her head up high and rounded the corner into the main cavern.

Jalthrax was standing in front of his birthmother when she saw him. As their eyes met, he spread his wings out as far as he could stretch them, already reaching four feet from tip to tip. Elody marveled at how big he was for just a baby.

Jalthrax let out a loud screech before flapping his wings and then finally settling down to walk slowly toward Elody. She smiled at his display and walked to meet him. As they met, he raised his head to her hand, and Elody dutifully rubbed down his neck. She couldn't stop smiling.

"He is ready," the Silver Queen said.

"Thank you for everything."

The Silver Queen smiled and nodded.

"Is there anything I should know before we leave?"

"You already know all that you need. You and Jalthrax will discover the rest as you grow."

"When will he be able to talk?"

"He will learn your language the more you speak to him. He can already understand some of the language of dragons, but he cannot speak it yet. It will come in time."

"Who will continue to teach him the dragon language?"

"Our tongue is the gift of Anarr. No one need teach it to him. He will come to know it on his own."

Elody looked again at Jalthrax, who was trying desperately to lead her hand to his neck, and couldn't believe how quickly he would change. He seemed so much like a baby to her now. But if the queen's words were to be believed, he might soon be talking to her.

"Thank you, Silver Queen."

She bowed and turned to leave, giving Jalthrax a little tug on his neck for him to follow. Over her shoulder she heard the Silver Queen say something in the growling tongue of the dragons. Jalthrax turned back to regard her for a moment before walking after Elody.

They left the cave together. Dragonmage and dragon.

Rinn was waiting outside the cave as his sister came out, and he saw Jalthrax for the first time walking behind her. He smiled at his sister and spread his arms to give her a big hug. She lowered her head and smiled back as he wrapped her in an embrace.

Jalthrax stretched his wings out wide and flapped them rapidly while screeching, blowing dirt and leaves all around them.

"Jalthrax, stop!" she said.

He lowered his body and drew his wings back to his side. He turned his head to the side to watch her and let out a low squawk. She and Rinn laughed and turned to leave.

"Come on," Rinn said. "Dad will be back from the ridge soon, and I'm anxious to hear the news. And everyone else will be excited to meet Jalthrax there."

"I'm just anxious to see that Dad is back safely."

Rinn nodded.

"Maybe we can go with him next time," Elody said. "I do have a dragon by my side."

She cast a look over her shoulder at Jalthrax who was walking a little behind her and craning his neck to look around. He moved his head quickly in different directions, taking in the world around him.

"I don't think Dad will let us go even with a dragon," Rinn said. "He wouldn't let me go even after I proved I can fight."

"None of the other boys went with the men either."

"I should fight with the men," Rinn said. "I'm eighteen already. I should have been fighting with the men two years ago, but Dad always makes me stay behind."

"Why?"

"To protect you," he said.

Elody bristled but quickly buried it. It wasn't Rinn's fault her father gave them the roles they had. He was only following her dad's orders.

"Well, I'll insist he include you next time. I have Jalthrax to protect me now."

Rinn looked back at the little dragon and chuckled.

"Some protection he is," Rinn said.

"Hey! He's still a dragon, you know."

Rinn ruffled her hair and smiled. They walked briskly

down the mountain path. The walk down was always faster than the walk up. Jalthrax stayed behind the two of them but would occasionally crane his neck forward and nudge Elody. She almost tripped and fell a few times, but she would just look over her shoulder and laugh.

"I'm sure he'll love meeting everyone if they're willing to feed him and rub on him," she said.

"He's like a big, winged dog."

"No he's not! He's nothing like a dog! He's still a baby, so he wants attention and touch, but he's not a dog."

"Okay, he's not a dog," Rinn said.

They walked in silence until they reached the bottom of the path. Once they hit the trees, Rinn drew his dagger and started twirling it anxiously in his hand.

"Stop it," Elody said. "You're making me nervous."

"Sorry."

He put the dagger away, but she saw his hand still hovering near it on his belt. She glanced around the trees, but she saw nothing. The three of them made an awful noise as they marched through the forest. The fall leaves beneath their feet crunched and crackled with every step. Elody had no doubt that if there were any goblins hiding, they'd have no trouble finding them.

"Should we let him hunt or get something to eat?" Rinn asked.

Elody stopped and turned around to look at Jalthrax. He tilted his head to the side and watched her as she stared at him.

"I don't know. I think he'll just fly off and hunt if he's

hungry."

The dragon straightened its head up and looked to the sky.

"Does he understand us?" Rinn asked.

"I don't know. Maybe some, I think. I didn't want to ask more questions and look dumb in front of the queen."

Rinn looked at the dragon who turned his head to meet his gaze.

"Are you hungry, Jalthrax?" he asked.

The dragon looked at him and then back up to the sky.

"Do you want to fly?" Elody asked.

He gave her a last look before he raised his wings, pumped them once, and lifted into the air. A few more flaps had him airborne and circling through the trees as he went higher and higher. He let out a loud screech as he soared up to the top of the forest.

"I guess he was hungry," Rinn said.

"I guess so."

They watched the sky as Jalthrax zipped between trees, screeching all the way. He was flying farther and farther from them and showed no signs of turning back.

"Well, what do we do now?" Rinn asked.

"I guess maybe we wait here for him to come back?"

"Can't he find you if we keep walking?"

"Yes, but I don't want him out here all alone."

"He's a dragon, El."

"I know, but he's still just a baby. I don't want to go back to the village without him. Everyone's expecting me to come home with a dragon."

Rinn walked over to a tree and sat down with his back against it.

"Might as well sit if we're gonna be here a while."

Elody looked at him and then back up to Jalthrax and watched as he disappeared from sight. With a sigh she went over and sat down next to him.

"I guess we wait," she said.

Chapter Ten

Fight

RINN SHIFTED IMPATIENTLY against the tree trunk and stood for the third time in as many minutes to scan the skies. He and Elody had been idly chatting for almost a half an hour with no sign of Jalthrax. With a huff, he sat back down and drew his dagger.

"How long is this going to take?" he asked.

"I don't know."

"It's not safe for us to be out here like this."

"Well, I didn't think he'd just fly off for hours."

Elody looked up and scanned the tops of the trees. After a minute of craning her neck, she slumped back down.

"I guess we can just go," she said. "He'll catch up to us."

"What about going home without a dragon?"

"I want to get home and make sure Dad is safe. Jalthrax can take care of himself."

Rinn didn't need anymore encouragement. He leapt up and wiped the dust and leaves from his hands and pants and then offered his hand to Elody. She took it and pulled herself off the ground and then brushed off her robes. She frowned.

"I wanted these to be perfect when I walked back into town," she said looking down at herself.

"Come here," Rinn said. "Turn around."

She turned around, and Rinn brushed the leaves and dirt off the backside of her robes.

"There," he said. "Now they look brand new."

She brushed a few more leaves from the front and smiled. They both looked up and searched the trees one last time. Nothing moved or made a sound.

"Come on, El."

Rinn turned and waited for her to move up alongside him before heading off. He hurried his steps trying to make up for the lost time, but he was careful not to let Elody fall behind him. The dry leaves crunched beneath their feet as they walked along the small trail that lead from the mountains back to their village.

They had only been walking a few minutes when they heard a screech from above. They both looked up to see Jalthrax flying swiftly through the trees and coming toward them.

"Finally," Rinn said.

They stopped walking and watched him fly closer. As he neared them, he let out a loud, frantic screech that echoed across the forest.

"Something's wrong," Rinn said.

Jalthrax's flying was erratic. He was dodging in and out of the trees at a breakneck pace. Rinn felt Elody grab his arm.

"What's wrong?" she said.

"I don't know."

Then he saw the arrows.

They arced through the air past Jalthrax as he flew behind a tree. Rinn snapped his gaze down and followed the path to see where they came from. A group of goblins had bows drawn and were taking aim with another round. He grabbed the sleeve of Elody's robe and yanked her to the ground as he rolled behind a tree.

"Goblins!"

Before he could grab her again, Elody stood up and yelled.

"Jalthrax!"

Rinn yanked her back down and snapped his finger to his lips with his eyes wide. But it was already too late. Arrows flew past where she was standing only a moment earlier, and he knew they had seen her. Rinn peeked his head around the tree to see where the goblins were. More arrows flew past as he pulled his head back.

Jalthrax let out another screech, and they looked up to see him flying down to where they were hiding. Rinn jumped up and tried to wave him off, but Jalthrax didn't seem to notice. He flew down and landed beside Elody amidst another volley of arrows.

"Get him down!" Rinn shouted.

Elody tugged on his neck and pulled him behind the tree where they were hiding. She had to turn him and press his wings against his body to get him behind cover, but she managed to get him hidden.

Rinn peeked around the tree again and saw the goblins had grouped together. They fanned out in a small line and started walking toward them. They were moving cautiously, but Rinn could see the wicked smiles on their faces.

"We have to run," Elody said.

"We can't run. They'll catch us and kill us all."

She bit her lip and pulled Jalthrax's head back down as he craned his neck up.

"We can't just stay here," she said.

Rinn didn't answer. He shut his eyes tightly and tried to think of something to do.

"Rinn!"

He turned to look at her. Elody was shaking. She was hugging Jalthrax close and pleading with her eyes.

"El. Did you learn the spell to throw your voice?"

"What?"

"In school, did you learn the spell to make your voice sound like it's coming from somewhere else?"

She shook her head.

"I didn't learn that one."

"Dammit. I don't know if I can do it still."

He took a deep breath and steadied himself.

"I want you to stay here," he said. "Don't move. Don't come out from behind the tree."

She nodded.

Rinn closed his eyes and breathed out slowly as he focused his mind inward. He hadn't attempted the spell in many years, and he didn't even know if he could pull enough power to complete it. He reached down inside himself and grasped for the well of magic within him.

Finding his magic had always been easy for Rinn, but he had never tried to cast under pressure like this. Even though that is what he was trained to do. He tried hard to ignore the sounds of the goblins getting nearer and the squeeze of Elody's hand on his leg. He pushed his mind down and found the magic.

In his thoughts, Rinn dipped his hands down and cupped them, trying to hold the magic and pull it up. It slipped through his fingertips. He took a deep breath and held it as he tried again. Spreading his fingers wide, he pushed down and felt the tingle. He grasped at it and pulled it to him.

Rinn opened his eyes and was calm. He could feel the magic in his fingers. His hands started moving as if on their own. As if they knew exactly what to do. He moulded the magic and shaped it into the spell he wanted. Casting such a simple spell took no time at all, but for Rinn, everything around him seemed to stand still.

Then, just like that, he was done. Did it work? Rinn cupped his hands around his mouth and focused on some trees over and behind the approaching goblins. Lowering his voice a bit, he shouted into his hands.

"This way, men! Archers, ready!"

Rinn heard his own voice echo back to him from across the trees and couldn't suppress a smile. He didn't know if the goblins understood him at all, but he guessed they must have, because the effect on them was instantaneous. They all turned and drew their bows back.

They held for a few seconds, trying to spot a target, but then shot at the trees themselves.

"Stay here," Rinn said over his shoulder.

He bolted from behind the tree and ran in the opposite direction the goblins were facing. They either didn't see him or paid him no attention. Either way, luck was on his side. He darted from tree to tree, always with an eye on them, and managed to get behind them. He cupped his hands to his mouth and focused on the other side of the goblins again.

"Archers, loose!" he shouted.

Rinn heard the twang of a bowstring and looked up with his eyes wide. A single arrow flew from the trees and thwacked into a goblin's chest with such force that it dropped him to the ground. The goblins all squealed and scrambled. They ducked and ran in all directions, most of them running into each other.

Another arrow flew through the air and struck one in the back, dropping him. Rinn's head darted from side to side trying to see where the arrows were coming from. It was the direction he had thrown his voice, but he saw no one. Who in the nine hells is shooting?

The goblins were in a panic now and running for cover. Some had gathered their wits enough to stop and shoot back, but having no target, they could only loose blindly into the trees. Another arrow flew, another goblin fell. The ones who had stopped to fight back were now on the run as well. And they were coming right toward Rinn.

He turned around and pressed his back to the tree

and waited for them to run by. He hoped none of them had seen him hiding as he heard their footsteps slowing. They started yelling at each other in goblin. Rinn dared a glance and saw that they had all stopped and ducked behind other trees and were watching the forest where the arrows had come from.

Rinn looked to where Elody was hiding and was thankful when he didn't see any part of her or Jalthrax sticking out. With his dagger in hand, he rolled quietly around the tree and snuck closer. The goblins were all facing the other direction and yelling at each other.

Rinn moved to the next tree, putting him right behind a goblin who was pressed against the tree in front of him. He took a deep, quiet breath and waited. The goblin shouted something back to another, and Rinn made his move. Quickly and quietly, he rolled around the tree and snuck up behind it. With a sharp thrust forward, he stabbed it in the back with his dagger and then pushed hard with his other hand, slamming its head into the tree.

Aside from the dull thud of its head hitting the tree, the goblin never made a sound. Rinn held his dagger for another few seconds before he let go and grabbed the body with both hands and laid it on the ground. He pulled his dagger out and wiped the blood on its loincloth before standing back up and looking around.

He heard the twang of a bowstring and several goblins shouting what he could only guess were curses. A couple of the goblins shot arrows from the trees they were hiding behind. Rinn watched as they all started dodging from tree to tree, getting closer to each other and regrouping. One of them shouted and looked back to where he was standing. He ducked back behind the tree and silently cursed himself and hoped they hadn't seen him.

Rinn heard a screech.

The goblins all went silent. Then he heard their footsteps slowly moving through the leaves. He waited several seconds before he dared a look. It was as he feared. The goblins were all moving from tree to tree toward where Elody and Jalthrax were hiding.

He cupped his hands to his mouth. Focusing his magic on the trees to the other side of the goblins, he let out the loudest battle cry he could. The goblins all jumped and turned at once, ready for a charge. Rinn darted around the tree and ran to the nearest one as fast as he could. It didn't have time to turn as he stabbed it in the back. He gave the dagger a twist and pulled it out.

"Elody, run!"

The goblins all turned at his shout and charged him. Rinn glanced down at the shortsword lying next to the dead goblin and thought for a moment to pick it up, but he knew it wouldn't do him any good. At least he would fight with the one weapon he knew how to use. He turned the dagger over in his hand and stood ready to meet them.

Six goblins came in a rush, moving faster than he'd ever seen any man move. Within a second they had all come together to charge in a tight group. Rinn stood his ground and didn't flinch. Elody has to escape. I have to protect her.

Another arrow flew from the trees and struck one in the back. It fell and got trampled by the one behind it who didn't stop its charge. Rinn gave a silent thanks to the unseen archer and readied himself. He shifted his weight from foot to foot as he rocked back and forth on his heels and swayed his dagger in front of him.

Then they were on him.

Rinn danced back as they all stabbed with their shortswords and managed to get out of their reach, but they pressed forward as a group. Rinn slashed out with his dagger and felt it bite into flesh. One of them screamed and pulled back, but the rest didn't even notice their companion.

Rinn jumped back as they all came in again, but he wasn't fast enough this time. He slashed out with his dagger and felt some satisfaction as he heard another scream, but the attack cost him. A sword pierced his side and cut through him, tearing a large gash that immediately began pouring blood.

Rinn screamed in pain and stumbled back. He fell hard against a tree and only just managed to remain standing. He pushed his feet out and used the tree to stand up straight, but through the pain he could see the goblins coming. He waved his dagger frantically, trying to keep them back.

They were moving more slowly toward him now, but even the two he had cut were still up and now moving in with the rest. He had hoped to kill a few of them before he died himself, but as they closed in around him, he gave up on that idea.

She's safe now. At least she's safe.

***

Elody ran as fast as she could.

She could hear and feel Jalthrax right behind her as she dodged around the trees in her way, and she knew he would be right there with her. Have to hurry. Not much time. Ahead of her she saw the goblins surrounding Rinn. She could see the blood pouring down his side, and she had to fight to choke back a scream.

She came around the last tree between her and the goblins and stopped. With anger and fear overwhelming her, she tried to take a deep breath and steady herself. Have to stay calm. She felt Jalthrax move up beside her and press his neck against her. In that instant, the fear was gone.

The rage bubbled over.

Elody closed her eyes and reached out her senses. She could feel Jalthrax next to her. Could feel his magic. It was radiating from him so strongly it was palpable. As if it were just there for her to take.

Elody reached out and immediately felt it in her hands. The force of it nearly knocked her back. It flowed into her and felt like it might overwhelm her. She reached up with her own hands and pushed back, pushing the dragon away from her.

The feeling of this magic was not the light, tingling feeling she was used to. The magic burned. It burned and felt as though it would burst from her fingertips in a great blast of raw energy. Elody flexed her fingers, and they felt tight.

She had to get this magic out of her.

When she opened her eyes, only a moment had passed, but she felt like she had blacked out. A quick survey of the scene in front of her brought her back to reality. She grasped the magic between her fingers and pulled it as she moved her hands in the pattern that would shape it into a spell.

She moved slowly at first but gained speed with each flick and twirl. Though she had never cast this spell with real magic behind it, she had practiced the motions for years until her master assured her she had them perfect. The magic within her fingers burned and pushed to get out.

With a final wave of her hands, she obliged.

The goblins were distracted when she first approached, but as she started casting, several of them turned. At the sight of the dragon beside her, they rushed in with a whoop and a yell. She must have seemed a perfect target. A helpless girl who wasn't even paying attention and a baby dragon. They ran at her with their swords leading the way.

Elody spread her fingers out in a fan and then dragged her hands in a wide arc that went from one side of her body to the next. Flames leapt from her fingertips as they passed, and the goblins could not stop their charge as they ran into them. They only had time to throw their arms up and scream before the flames fell over them. The magical fire burned hot and fast and lit them all like torches.

Elody stood with her hands ready and waited for them all die. But the fire did not kill the goblins right away. They stumbled back, screaming in agony as the flames consumed their flesh. Elody heard their screams and smelled their burning flesh and recoiled in horror.

They fell to the ground screaming and tried to beat the fire off of them, but the magical flames would not be extinguished. Elody turned away and brought her hand to her mouth. She didn't look at them, but she could hear their continued screams.

She didn't know what to do, but she couldn't just stand there. She twisted around and started forward thinking she could put the flames out. But just as quickly, the screaming stopped, and the goblins laid still. Their bodies continued to burn, but Elody couldn't watch anymore.

She remembered Rinn.

Her eyes went from the dead goblins to Rinn slumped against the tree where she had seen him bleeding only a moment ago. She never stopped to see where the other goblins were, she just leapt over the corpses and ran to him.

"Rinn!"

He didn't move. His eyes were closed, and his shirt and pants were covered in blood.

"Rinn!"

She shook his shoulders, but his head just rolled listlessly and slumped down. She grabbed him in a hug and squeezed him to her.

"Wake up, Rinn!"

"Get away, girl!"

Her eyes snapped open as she let go of Rinn and stood up. A man ran toward them. She started to say something, but he pushed past her and knelt down. He touched Rinn's neck and then slid his hands underneath him.

"What are you doing?" she yelled.

"He's still alive, but he won't be for long, now move!"

The man picked Rinn up with a strength she would not have guessed for his small frame. The man struggled for a moment but managed to get Rinn up and into his arms. And just like that, he was off and running.

Elody had no choice but to run after him.

CHAPTER ELEVEN

A CABIN IN THE WOODS

ELODY STRUGGLED TO keep up even as the man was carrying Rinn's extra weight. She didn't know where they were going, but the man seemed to. He wasn't running, but he moved in and out of the trees with such grace and confidence that Elody actually lost sight of him a few times. Jalthrax was right behind her and following her every step. She moved around another tree and saw him up ahead.

She sped up as much as she dared and managed to close the distance enough to keep up with him. Then, just as suddenly, he was gone. One minute she could see the back of him with Rinn's head and legs lolling to either side. The next, he disappeared. She ran toward the last place she saw him and then stopped in her tracks.

As she reached the spot where he had disappeared, the trees suddenly seemed to part and open up to a small clearing and a cabin in the woods. She knew she had not seen the cabin a moment ago, even while running just a few feet back. Rinn was laying on the ground just outside, and the door was swung open. Jalthrax moved alongside her as she ran to him.

She knelt down and started to remove his shirt. It had already been torn open to reveal the gash in his side, and she felt her breath catch as she saw it. *It's bad.* She could see parts of his insides peeking out, and the blood was still pouring out, though slower now. She felt Jalthrax beside her as he dropped his head and laid still.

Elody had seen wounds like this before. *He won't live.* She tried hard to be brave. Shaking the tears from her face, she grabbed his shirt and pulled it out from under him. She took his dagger and started cutting and tearing the shirt into strips. *If he was going to die, it wasn't going to be because she sat there and let him.*

"He's dying!" she cried out.

The man appeared in an instant and ran out. He knelt down in front of Rinn and dropped a leather pouch beside him. He reached in and grabbed a small pot with a lid on it and shoved it into her hands.

"Apply this to the wound," he said.

Elody didn't ask.

She opened it up and stuck her fingers into the thick goop that it contained. She was hit with a smell like fish and honey. It nearly made her gag, but she did as she was told. Taking a handful, she rubbed it gently over the wound. It turned burnt orange between her fingers as it mixed with Rinn's blood.

"Quickly, girl."

She shot him an angry look, but he wasn't paying attention. He had reached into the pouch and pulled out a small vial of a crystal blue liquid. Without ceremony, he popped the small cork and pushed it to Rinn's lips. He yanked his head off the ground and poured a small amount of the contents down his throat.

Rinn's body twitched beneath her hands, and she pulled away as he started to convulse. The man grabbed the bandages she had torn and shoved them into her hands.

"Bind it," he said.

Elody grabbed the strips of shirt and pressed them into the ointment on his wound where they stuck fast. She started to push some of the longer bandages under him to tie it off.

"He won't need that. Keep your hands tight on him."

He grabbed Rinn's head and poured more of the vial down his throat. He started to sputter and cough.

"You're choking him!"

"There's a spring behind the cabin and a bucket next to it. Go and fetch some water."

"I'm not leaving him—"

"Fetch some water!"

Elody jumped up and ran to the back of the cabin. She found the bucket sitting on the ground next to a small pool of bubbling water. With a quick yank, she picked it up and filled it with water and then ran back to the front to see the man pouring the remainder of the vial into Rinn's mouth.

She knelt down beside him and watched. Rinn's body had stopped moving, and he was lying peacefully. His chest rose and fell with deep breaths. She looked at the man, and he raised his eyes to meet hers for only a second before looking back down.

Rinn's eyes blinked, slowly at first, and then shot open in surprise. He tried to push off the ground, but the man had his hands on him and pushing him back down before Elody even registered what was happening.

"Stay down, you fool! Your wound isn't mended yet."

The man's arms looked small, but he easily held Rinn down. With one arm across his chest, the man reached down with the other and touched the bandages, poking them gently.

"Lie still and let the ointment do its work."

Rinn nodded his head and turned to look at his sister.

"Why didn't you run?" he said.

"Because you needed me."

"I was trying to let you escape."

"And I was trying to let you live."

"What happened? I remember getting cut, and then I hit a tree. I tried to fight them off, but I blacked out."

"I killed them," she said.

Rinn looked at her, but she looked down.

"All of them?" he asked.

"Most of them," she said. "I don't know what happened to the rest. They must've run."

"None of the goblins escaped," the man said.

They both turned to look at him, but he was looking at Rinn's wounds. He prodded the bandages again and then pressed lightly.

"Better," he said. "Sit up a little now and drink some water."

Rinn slowly sat up on his elbows and then the man helped him to a sitting position. Elody leaned the bucket of water to his lips where he started gulping.

"Slowly," the man said.

Rinn drained half the bucket and wiped his mouth. He looked down at himself and then back up in confusion.

"What happened to my shirt?"

"We needed it," she said. "It was already ruined from the blood."

He put his hand to his side and felt the wound. He winced as he pushed on it, but only a little. He looked down at the blood-soaked bandage and then back up to the man.

"You saved my life," he said.

"I couldn't let you die."

"You were the one shooting at the goblins," Elody said.

He nodded.

"I heard the dragon and followed him back to you as the goblins were tracking him," he said.

At his mention, Jalthrax picked his head up and looked at them.

"Thank you," Elody said.

He nodded, and his hair fell down in front of his face. Elody noticed his ears for the first time. They were pointed at the top. She looked over his face and found that it was very soft, more like a woman than a man, but the stubble of his beard covered it.

"You're an elf," she said.

He looked up at her.

"Half," he said.

"I'm Elody, and this is my brother, Rinn."

"Eryninn."

She smiled at him, but he didn't return it.

"What is your dragon's name?" he asked.

"Oh, I forgot. This is Jalthrax."

"He is one of the Silver Queen's, yes?"

"Yes."

Eryninn nodded his head and reached out toward the dragon. Jalthrax pulled his head back for a moment and then leaned forward to let his hand touch him. Eryninn held his hand gently on his head before sliding to the side and stroking his neck. Jalthrax closed his eyes, and a low growl escaped his lips. Elody laughed and saw a little smile cross Eryninn's lips, but it disappeared just as quickly.

"I think he likes you," she said.

"I have a way with dragons."

"We need to go," Rinn said suddenly.

Eryninn took his hand away from the dragon and stood up.

"We need to get home," Rinn said.

"You're wounded," Eryninn said.

"I feel no pain. My wound is almost healed, thanks to you. I only wish that we could repay you, but we must get home."

"The woods may not be safe just now," Eryninn said.

"The whole village is expecting our return," Elody said. "Our dad will worry."

Rinn started to rise, and Eryninn extended his hand down to help him up. Rinn grasped it and pulled himself up.

"We have to get back to the village," Rinn said.

Eryninn shook his head and sighed.

"Then I will escort you," he said.

"Why would you do that?" Rinn asked.

"It wouldn't do much good to save your life only to let you run off alone."

"Do you think it is that dangerous?" Elody asked.

"I've been patrolling the woods more frequently, but your attack and mine are the only ones I've witnessed. Perhaps they are just hungry. We are approaching winter when the goblin tribes grow more desperate. Or perhaps they are just hungry for blood."

Elody couldn't suppress a shudder.

"Give me a moment," the half-elf said.

He turned and went inside the cabin. They waited for him for a minute without a sound from inside. Elody looked at Rinn who only shrugged. She shuffled over to stand in the doorway and peer inside.

Eryninn was moving around and grabbing things from the cabin. He picked up a few small things Elody couldn't see and stuffed them into a pack. Then he grabbed several quivers of arrows that were leaning against the wall and tossed them onto the bed.

He stopped in front of a green, hooded cloak that hung from a hook on the wall. Shaking his head, he stared at it. With a slow hand, he reached up and touched it. He ran his fingers gently down its length and ruffled the bottom before taking it off the hook. He held it a moment more before he slung it around his neck and clicked the little clasp together. He pulled the hood up over his head and went back to his work gathering things.

"You're the wood elf, aren't you?" Elody said.

He glanced at her and his steps slowed for a moment, but he said nothing. She watched him open the top drawer of a small dresser and take something from it and place it in a pouch on his belt.

"A girl in our village was saved by the wood elf once. She was nearly killed by a bear, but the wood elf frightened it off."

He said nothing. Just swept around the little cabin without looking back at her. Finally, he picked up a shortsword in a scabbard that hung from a post on the small bed and buckled it around his waist. He grabbed up his pack and walked out, pulling the door closed behind him.

"I'm done here," he said.

He pushed past her and reached into his pack for something. Pulling his hand out, he tossed a shirt at Rinn.

"It might be a bit tight, but it should fit," Eryninn said.

"Um, thanks," Rinn said.

The half-elf passed him without a look and knelt down to grab the pouch he had left on the ground. He scooped up the little clay jar and the ointment that remained and shoved them into the pouch and then stuffed it into his pack. Jalthrax moved next to him and tried to nuzzle him, but he gently pushed him away as he stood.

"You are him, aren't you?" Elody said.

"Who?" her brother said, pulling the shirt over his head.

"No," he said as he walked past her to the edge of the clearing.

"But you have to be," she said. "You saved us. And the cloak, the bow, the sword. They all match the tales."

"My father was the one you call the wood elf. These are his things."

"Oh," she said.

"We should get going," he said.

He started walking before Rinn even had a chance to stand up. Elody helped him up and shrugged. They collected themselves and jogged after him with Jalthrax in tow.

Chapter Twelve

A Village Burning

ELODY AND RINN ran close behind Eryninn. The half-elf stayed ahead of them and would occasionally stop to check the ground or a tree. Rinn would stop and examine whatever Eryninn did before jogging to catch up. Elody would look too but gave up after a few times of seeing nothing at all and fell back behind them.

The two of them ahead of her made very little noise as they walked, but she was no good at keeping quiet. Jalthrax was even worse. He sounded like a barrel rolling through the forest, crushing every leaf and breaking every branch in his path. She tried to silence him with a finger or a look, but he would only squawk back at her, so she gave up. Rinn and Eryninn had stopped ahead of her and were kneeling on the ground as she jogged to catch up. Eryninn threw her an annoyed glance as Jalthrax came stomping up.

"He'd be quiet if he flew," she said.

"No," Eryninn said, "he'll be spotted too easily."

He looked down and touched the ground, pointing to

light impressions in the soil.

"More goblin sign," he said. "Footprints there and there. Very recent."

"More like the ones we killed?" Rinn asked.

"Could be. One goblin foot is as ugly as the next."

Rinn looked up and around the forest.

"We're getting close to the village. We're not more than a half-hour walk from our farm."

The half-elf touched the ground again and then looked around the trees.

"Too close," he whispered.

Elody leaned in for a closer look, but Eryninn stood and kept going. He marched toward the village at a faster pace than before, and Elody hurried her steps to keep up. She saw him glance around nervously as they walked. He was being subtle with his movements, but she saw him slide his bow from his shoulder and carry it in his hand.

"You know something," she said as she scooted closer to him.

He didn't acknowledge her. Just quickened his pace. Elody jogged a few steps to move beside him and then walked in step.

"What do you know?"

He kept walking.

Rinn had moved up to his other side. When Eryninn wouldn't look at them, Rinn stepped in front of him. The half-elf pulled up short and looked at them.

"What do you know?" Elody asked.

He stared hard at them both.

"I had thought these tracks were from a hunting party," he said, "but there are far too many for that."

"What does that mean?" Elody asked.

"Goblins haven't come this far out of their holes in many, many years. And never in numbers like this. I've seen enough years to have witnessed goblin raids on small villages like yours. It doesn't turn out well for the villagers."

"You think a goblin tribe is coming to attack our village?" Elody said.

"A tribe maybe you could handle. This is more than one by the looks of it."

Elody had moved around to stand beside her brother.

"I didn't think goblin tribes joined together," Rinn said.

"They don't," Eryninn said. "That is what worries me the most."

"Our village is well defended," Elody said.

"Against a tribe, maybe," Eryninn said. "Not this. Not this many."

"What else can we do but fight?" Rinn said. "Our village is strong. We can beat them back."

"Maybe you will," Eryninn said. "Maybe you'll kill them all, and maybe you'll do it without losing a man. More likely the whole village will be slaughtered."

Rinn clenched his fists until they went white.

"How can you say that?" he yelled.

"Because it is the truth."

Rinn looked at her, too stunned to even speak.

"There is no time to stand around," Eryninn said. "I

might be wrong about all this, but standing here won't help anyone."

He didn't wait for them. Rinn and Elody followed him toward the village. Toward home. Jalthrax was right behind her. Elody prayed silently as they ran on.

Please be wrong.

He had to be wrong. They were just old tracks, or they were the same goblins crisscrossing their own path.

This was supposed to be her day. The day she brought home her dragon. Her father was waiting for them to come home with Jalthrax. He has to be wrong. This can't be happening.

Not today.

***

Rinn could see the smoke rising above the trees long before he could see the village. He ran faster even as he heard Eryninn call out for him to wait. He came to a stop at the edge of the trees just on the outskirts of the village.

He pressed close behind a tree and watched while the rest caught up to him and stopped. As they all tried to catch their breath, they stared down into the village.

Or what was left of it.

Most of the homes and buildings had been burned to the ground. The smoke was thick in the air as the remains smoldered. They heard screams pierce the air, but they couldn't see anyone. From their vantage point in the trees, they could see the bodies littering the ground everywhere.

They were too late.

Elody cried out softly and put her hand to her mouth. Rinn's whole body trembled. His fist clenched around the hilt of his dagger, though he didn't remember even drawing it.

Goblins were moving through the village in small groups collecting valuables and piling up everything they could find. They stepped over the mangled, burnt bodies of the dead villagers around them. Some were going around and stabbing the corpses where they laid. Rinn jumped as Elody touched his arm.

He snapped a look at Elody, and her eyes suddenly went wide.

"Dad," she said.

It took a second for the word to register. Rinn pulled out of her grip and ran from the trees toward their farm.

"Wait, Rinn!" she shouted.

But he wasn't listening.

He ran as fast as he could. Ahead of him, their farmhouse was burning. He could hear Elody and Jalthrax running far behind him, but he didn't wait for them to catch up. Rinn tore around the side of the house and stopped in his tracks.

There were bodies everywhere.

Bodies of men and goblins alike. They covered the ground and soaked it with blood. Too many to even count. How could there be so many?

Rinn caught sight of movement. Walking amongst the dead was a group of three goblins. They were checking the dead and stabbing the corpses of each man as they passed.

Rinn's rage overwhelmed him. Without a sound, he charged. He heard Elody shout from somewhere behind him.

"Rinn, stop!"

Rinn kept running.

The goblins looked up at the commotion and started to scramble. Rinn got to them first. He hit the first one running, slamming it with his shoulder, and knocking it to the ground. Two more charged him as his momentum slowed.

Rinn slashed at the nearest goblin. It knocked his dagger aside. The one in back moved around to flank him. He heard an arrow whistle past his ear and saw it thunk into the second one's chest, throwing it back and to the ground. The other goblin turned to look behind it and then turned back with its eyes wide.

Rinn leapt in with the distraction and stabbed it in the gut just as it turned back to face him. He kicked out with his boot and knocked the stunned creature to the ground where it thrashed and screamed. Behind him, he heard the goblin he shoulder blocked getting up and yelling. He spun around and saw another arrow silence it as it pierced his throat.

The one on the ground was still screaming and shouting in goblin. Seeing that it had dropped its sword in all its flailing, Rinn walked to it and slammed his boot down on its head. It thrashed around some more, so he slammed his boot down again. And again. The goblin was still after the second stomp, but Rinn couldn't stop. Over and over again he raised his foot and brought it down on its head, splattering it. From somewhere behind him he heard Elody scream, and it shook him.

"DADDY!"

Rinn twisted around.

Elody was kneeling on the ground a few feet away, cradling his father's bloody head in her hands. Rinn's anger slipped away in the instant it took him to understand what he saw. His whole body went weak as he tried to move. He took slow, heavy steps toward her, fighting with each one to stay upright. His knees quivered, and a scream caught in his tightening throat. His dagger fell from his hand as he crumbled to his knees beside her.

Rinn fell over his father and cried. Elody reached out and took his hands. Neither could stop the tears or the wails that escaped their lips. Their bodies shook and convulsed with the pain and sobs. Rinn screamed into his father's still chest and cried out, and Elody only cried harder.

Through the tears, Rinn opened his eyes and saw Jalthrax lying on the ground a few feet away. Eryninn was standing stiffly next to him and watching all around them. When their eyes met, Rinn blinked back the tears and saw the half-elf's eyes soften for a moment before he looked away. Eryninn kept watch over them, never making a sound.

Rinn picked his head up and looked at Elody who was wiping the tears from her cheeks only to have them replaced when her face quivered and the crying started all over again. He laid his hands over hers on their father's chest and squeezed them. Rinn didn't know how long they stayed like that, but it seemed like minutes passed with neither of them moving. He looked up when he felt a tug on his shoulder.

"There is no more time for this now," Eryninn said.

Rinn's jaw tightened. He clenched his hands into fists, nearly crushing his sister's delicate fingers. He pushed himself to his feet and turned sharply to face the half-elf.

"Our father is dead!" Rinn shouted.

"There are many more than that and more still to come. We must go."

"Go? We can't go! We can't just let our friends die! We have to fight!"

"We can't just leave these people!" Elody said.

She fought with her robes and struggled to get to her feet as she moved to stand beside her brother. Eryninn breathed a heavy sigh and pulled his bow over his shoulder.

"This is not a fight," he said. "This is a slaughter. There is nothing you can do here but die next to these people."

"We can't just leave everyone to die!" Rinn shouted.

Their tears had been wiped away now, replaced by anger. Jalthrax was still lying quietly in the grass, never taking his eyes from Elody. She turned back to look at her dead father, and the tears started again. She fell to her knees and sobbed. Rinn looked at Eryninn, his eyes pleading for an answer.

"You can't fight this back," he said. "There are too many of them."

"You're a coward!" Rinn said.

Their eyes locked in a grim stare.

"You need to protect your sister now."

Rinn held his gaze and wiped the tears away, but he did not budge. Eryninn turned his eyes to Elody who was kneeling on the ground and moaning, holding her father's hand. Rinn looked down to her again and then back up at him.

"Come on, Elody," Rinn said. "We have to go."

He wiped his eyes on the sleeve of his shirt and pulled her to her feet. With a last look back, they ran. They ran back into the forest and away from the smoke and the screams of their dying friends.

***

Elody stumbled many times in their run from the village, but she managed to stay on her feet and not fall too far behind. She kept looking back over her shoulder expecting goblins to be chasing them, but she never saw anything. Jalthrax flew above them, his shadow always where Elody could see it.

Once they were far enough from the village, they all stopped to rest and catch their breaths. They each found a tree to lean against and slid to the ground heaving and panting. Jalthrax flew down and landed softly between them.

They rested in silence for several minutes until the heavy breathing had stopped. Eryninn passed around a water skin, and they all drank heavily.

"Let's get moving," he said.

Elody pushed off the ground and managed to stand, but her legs quivered in protest. She didn't know if she could keep running.

"We need to be more cautious from here," Eryninn said. "There may be goblins still lurking in the forest."

They set off again.

Slowly but steadily, they made their way through the forest to the cabin. Eryninn jogged out ahead of them and scanned the forest around them as they walked. The going was slower, and Elody was thankful for it. Jalthrax was walking along with her now, and she found herself touching him for support more than once. She could feel a little surge of energy every time her hand brushed his skin.

They had walked for more than half an hour when Eryninn suddenly disappeared ahead of them. One second he was walking cautiously in front of them, and in the next blink he was gone. Just like before. Rinn swung his head around to look at Elody, and they both shrugged. Rinn kept walking to where they last saw him, and just as suddenly, he was gone.

"Rinn!" Elody shouted.

"What?" he called back.

She could hear him as clear as if he were standing there, but he was nowhere to be seen.

"Where ... Where did you go?"

"I'm right here. I'm looking at you."

Elody looked all around but saw nothing. She walked to where Rinn had just disappeared, and in an instant the forest in front of her changed. Rinn appeared so quickly that she nearly ran into him. Behind him was Eryninn's cabin. But it hadn't been there just a moment ago.

"Come," Eryninn said.

They both looked up to see him coming around the side of the house with a bucket full of water. He grabbed a ladle and dipped it in, pouring it over his head and down his face. He went back for another dip and drank it down in quick gulps.

They both stood in stunned silence looking around them. They walked over and collapsed to the ground before grabbing the ladle and drinking heavily.

"What is this place?" Rinn asked.

"This was my home as a child," Eryninn said.

"How can we not see it from the forest?"

"It is protected from eyes I do not wish to see it. My father created the enchantment to protect my mother when he was away."

Rinn only nodded.

They sat in silence for several minutes. Jalthrax had curled up next to Elody and put his head in her lap. Petting him gave her some distraction, but it wasn't enough.

As she thought about her father and her village, she could feel the pain all over again. She hadn't had time to think about it while they were running for their lives, but now that everything was quiet, it all came flooding back. She buried her head in her knees and rocked slowly back and forth.

She looked at Rinn, but he did not meet her eyes. He stared off into the forest with a blank expression and said nothing. Elody fought several times to stop crying and lost each time. She shook her head and growled through the tears, brushing them away.

Don't be a child.

Stroking Jalthrax had a calming effect on her. Every time her hand touched his leathery skin she felt better. When she finally stopped crying, she leaned down and gently kissed his head. He lifted it and looked at her for a moment and then settled back into her lap.

"What do we do?" her brother asked, breaking the silence.

"We hide here for a bit and figure it out," Eryninn said.

"What is there to figure out?" Rinn said.

"Our next move," Eryninn said.

"We have no moves!" Rinn shouted. "Our village is dead. Our father is dead. We should have been there. We could have beaten them if Elody and I had been there with Jalthrax."

"Your village never stood a chance," Eryninn said.

"We could have fought! We could have saved someone! We could have saved my dad!"

"You would have died right along with him!"

Elody's head shot up when she heard Eryninn yell. He took two quick steps and stood over Rinn.

"You listen to me. Your village was doomed. The minute those goblins decided to take it, there was nothing you or anyone else here could do."

Rinn leapt to his feet and stared hard at the half-elf. He opened his mouth several times to speak but could not find the words. Rinn turned his back and stomped away. He stared back into the forest for a while before speaking again.

"Why did they do this?" Rinn asked.

"Goblins don't need a reason," Eryninn said.

Rinn spun around to face him.

"You must have something they want," Eryninn said.

"We're just farmers and hunters. We don't even have a proper tavern!"

"They wanted something."

"The Silver Queen!" Elody suddenly shouted.

They both looked up to see her bright eyes wide with an idea. She jumped up and ran to them.

"That's not why they came," Eryninn said. "Believe me, goblins want no part of that dragon."

"No, that's just it!" Elody said. "I don't know what they're here for, but one thing they definitely don't want is to face her. She can help us!"

"What's to help?" her brother asked. "The village is burned, and everyone's dead by now."

"Not everyone," Eryninn said. "Goblins don't kill everyone. They save some for having fun. Most of the men will be dead, but there might be some women or children left alive."

"Dragon mothers often protect the towns they nest near," Elody said. "We can go to the queen and ask her to help! She could swat down an army of goblins!"

It would work. The Silver Queen was old and large even for her kind. She could extinguish the fires in the village and kill the entire goblin force in one great blast of her freezing breath.

"The Silver Queen will not help you," Eryninn said.

"That is not her way."

"She will!" Elody said. "I know she will help us!"

"It's worth a shot," her brother said.

Eryninn shook his head.

"She will not fight for you," he said softly.

Now Elody's anger bubbled over.

"Well, who else can we ask?" she yelled. "Your father? Are the elves going to come and help us? Are you going to fight an entire goblin horde by yourself?"

She couldn't control her shouting. She needed to do something to help her village. Her plan would work. She had spent time with the queen, befriended her even.

She will help us.

Eryninn kept silent. She detected a hint of sadness in his eyes as he stared at her. He dropped his gaze and nodded with a sigh.

"Okay," he said.

"She will help us," Elody said.

Rinn went to the bucket and took another drink of water and then turned back. Elody moved up beside him, and they both looked at Eryninn who was looking down and shaking his head.

"Thank you for everything," Rinn said.

"We would not be alive without your help," Elody said.

Jalthrax moved alongside them as they left the clearing. Once they were clear of the grove, he flapped his wings and flew into the air above them. They used him as a guide and followed his path into the mountains. They had walked for several minutes before Elody felt someone behind her.

"This is a waste of a trip," she heard Eryninn say.

She hadn't caught his footsteps or even a sound as he had run to catch up with them, but she smiled to herself when she heard his voice.

"Then why are you coming?" she asked.

"Because without me, you have no chance of convincing her to help you."

Elody never looked back.

She will help us.

CHAPTER THIRTEEN

TO KILL A QUEEN

SHE FELT THE presence long before she heard the footsteps echo off the walls of the cave. Kiranoth, the Silver Queen, was an old dragon. She had lived hundreds of years and fought through too many wars. She could feel the power that approached.

The elf was thinner and smaller than she expected. His slight form gave no hint of the power she felt from him. Kiranoth had risen to her full height in the cave and had spread her wings out to stretch them. She sensed the magic around him and knew that he had many enchantments cast upon himself.

He was not here for a chat.

"Greetings, Kiranoth'ul'Daltharr," the elf said. "I am Velanon."

She was not used to being called by her proper name except in the ceremony of the dragonmages. The elf bowed, but she knew it was no sign of respect. Kiranoth stared down at him in silence.

"Do you know who I am?" he said.

"You are the one who has been slaying my kind."

"I am."

It was no surprise to her. Kiranoth had many friends among the elves, and they often came to visit. Some even wizards. But never with power like this emanating from them.

"Then you know why I am here," Velanon said.

Kiranoth stood perfectly still. *Think.* She had heard rumors of some of the dragons this one had killed. Some even older than her. She could flee, but he would catch her. It would be a fight then.

"If you have a clutch, I will allow you to remove them," he said.

Kiranoth could hardly keep the disdain from her voice.

"So that you might keep them for yourself? I would sooner crush them beneath my own claws."

The elf frowned and shook his head.

"A pity. They would have made fine pets."

Kiranoth narrowed her eyes and glared down at the little elf. She wanted nothing more than to lift a single claw and crush the life from his tiny body. From head to toe he was not as long as one of her talons. But she knew better than to underestimate him.

He is hiding something.

Elves lived for many hundreds of years. She knew from experience that they could gain an extraordinary amount of power in their long lifetime. There was no telling how old this one was. It could be that he was incredibly arrogant, but she knew that his confidence must be at least partly earned.

He made no move to attack or cast a spell. Just stood there looking at her.

"What have I done to deserve to die?" she finally asked.

"You and your greedy kin have done more than enough to deserve the death of all dragonkind. Your death is but a single one in a long line of dead dragons."

"So, you hunt dragons for fun?"

"No. I do not hunt your kind for sport or challenge. None that I have killed thus far have given me either. I will hunt you and your kin to extinction just as your kind hunted mine. I am merely restoring a balance that was broken."

Kiranoth eyed him curiously. She sensed an anger bubbling behind his even tone.

"I have never hunted elves or any of mankind. My bonded parent was an elf for nearly all of my life."

"Not elves, wyrm. My kind was once plentiful throughout the world before you and your kind hunted them down. Men wielded true power without the aid of dragons. We called to the magic with our voices."

"You speak of wizards. I have never directly harmed a wizard to my knowledge."

"Then you shall pay a price for the actions of your kind."

"We have no quarrel with wizards."

"You should study your history, wyrm. I have. Dragons started a war and hunted and killed the wizards in order to make themselves the only beings that could wield magical power in the world. Did you never wonder where they all went? With the voice of magic silenced, the dragons have little to fear from mankind."

"You speak of a war between dragons and wizards that was so long ago it has fallen from the pages of history. That it was dragons who silenced the song of magic for our own vanity and power. Even if all that you say is true, I have never hunted a wizard or man of any kind. Yet you are here to murder an innocent for the alleged wrongs of my ancestors?"

"I am."

Kiranoth lowered her gaze and shook her mighty head.

"You shame the race of elves."

"The elves are not my people, lizard. My people were murdered by dragons long before I was born."

His demeanor was calm, but Kiranoth could see the anger simmering behind his eyes. There was no use in arguing. She had no illusions that she could dissuade the elf from his intended course. She only wished to know his reason and stall for time to prepare herself for the coming battle.

With a motion quicker than one would expect from a creature her size, Kiranoth stretched out and swept her mighty claw at him.

He stood motionless. Fearless.

As her claw neared his body, she felt it hit an unseen force and rebound back. Even with all of her mighty strength behind the attack, it turned aside as if she'd hit an immovable wall. But there was nothing there. She sensed no barrier before her.

Velanon took only a moment to meet her gaze. The calm expression on his face never changed. He began moving his hands and chanting. The ancient words of magic flowed from his lips with practiced ease, and his hands moved in perfect motion. Kiranoth had known many wizards in her life. She had heard the language of magic spoken aloud before. Some of the oldest dragons still spoke it.

Kiranoth took a giant breath that seemed to suck all of the air from the cave. Pausing for only a split second as her lungs filled, she blew a great blast of ice and frost. The elf finished his movement only a moment before and then stood motionless again.

The great dragon's breath should have frozen his bones where they stood, but it never got near him. The blizzard blew and swirled around him but fell against a barrier and parted harmlessly to the side.

Kiranoth was stunned, but she didn't let it show. Velanon's face was a sea of calm. She was playing right into his hands. The wizard was prepared for her every move.

The elf started chanting again and moved his hands in quick, practiced motions. Kiranoth was not waiting around to see what would spring forth. Using the innate powers of her kind, she summoned forth a cloud of fog that rolled in as if from nowhere and blanketed the entire cave.

He completed his spell and flung his hands toward her head. A giant ball of fire exploded, and the magical fires burned away the flog at the top of the cave. But she was gone.

Kiranoth could see perfectly through the fog cloud she had created even as she now watched them through elven eyes. Her form was too big to do battle in the cave. She had shifted to that of an elven maiden. But she did not shift fast enough to escape the wizard's fire entirely.

The side of her face was badly burned, and she was glad for the fog cloud hiding her. She did not want the elf to know he had wounded her already.

She needed more time.

***

Velanon did not hide the surprise on his face when his fireball exploded seemingly into nothing. He had never fought a silver dragon before, but he had read every tome he could find on them. The old girl was too big to have just walked or flown out of the cave without hearing it, so he knew she must have changed forms.

"I came to fight a dragon, not a girl or a donkey or whatever you've become," he said.

Velanon shouted through the fog, but no answer came back. *She's still here. I can feel here.* She could have escaped through the back of the cave, but he had not fought a dragon yet who took the opportunity to escape.

Even when so obviously overmatched.

With a few words and a quick movement, Velanon summoned a great gust of wind from his hands. The fog cloud swirled violently and was dispersed. An elven maiden stood at the rear of the cave, just beyond the fog.

Velanon started to say something, but the elf maiden

raised her hand to point at him, and a cone of freezing cold ice flew at him. He jumped quickly to the side to avoid the blast, but he still caught most of it. The spells he had prepared on himself before entering the cave absorbed some of the cold but not all of it. He still felt the bitter chill.

Velanon pushed himself up off the ground and snarled before starting another spell. He launched a second fireball at the elf who was already starting to run for the back exit of the cave. Perhaps she's smarter than she looks. The flaming sphere reached her and exploded in a giant, fiery cloud that engulfed her.

He smiled when he heard a satisfying scream from across the cave, but it quickly disappeared. He could still feel the ice that clung to his clothes and froze his skin. He was not taking a chance of feeling that cold bite again.

The words of magic flowed from his lips, and his hands flew through the air in rapid circles. He dared a glance at the dragon in her elven form and saw that she too was in the throes of casting.

**

Kiranoth was deep in concentration with her spell, but she could hear the words floating across the cave. She knew the wizard was casting too. She had to finish her spell first.

She should have guessed that the wizard would have warded himself against cold. She hoped he had little such protection from fire. Kiranoth finished casting and flung her spell across the cavern.

As she let loose, she looked across the cavern to see the elf finish his spell as well. She saw her fireball explode, and the elf fall to the side, but not before releasing something from his hand. A tiny, orange ball, no bigger than a marble, shot across the cave toward her. She tried to turn and run down her exit tunnel in the back of the cave, but she wasn't fast enough.

The tiny ball exploded into a giant cloud of fire much bigger than the previous fireballs the wizard had thrown. She dove to the ground trying to cover herself from the flames, but it did little good.

Fire was no friend to her kind.

She curled her elven form into a ball, but the fires burned so hot and so long. Her bare skin began to blister and sizzle.

As the fires died away, Kiranoth rolled to her stomach and tried to push herself to stand. Her elven body was weak and badly burned, but she knew she would only present a bigger target in her true form. She stood to meet the wizard with a spell on her lips, but it died away quickly as a bolt of lightning struck her in the chest. It blasted her against the cave wall, and she cried out.

When her body stopped twitching, she could barely move. She uncurled and tried to roll over. Pain shot through every part of her. Pain she had never felt in all her years.

She heard footsteps approaching and knew her time had come.

"You never stood a chance, lizard. I came prepared to counter your every move, yet still you fought. It would be admirable if not born out of arrogance and ego. You dragons are all alike."

Kiranoth turned her eyes upward to stare hard at the elf. His clothes were smoldering, and his face was badly burned. She smiled.

"You don't look as prepared as you think."

The air in her lungs felt heavy. It took great effort to speak, and she felt as if she was inhaling fire with every breath.

Velanon chuckled and pulled his burnt cloak around to admire the damage.

"Yes, you got a bit lucky. I shall have to remember that the next time. You are much smarter than some of your kin."

Her breaths were coming in short bursts now. Kiranoth closed her eyes and willed herself to change. To revert back to her true form.

She would not die like this.

He saw her body begin to shift and moved back quickly before he was crushed beneath her massive form. Her skin turned silvery and started to expand out very quickly until it became small and then larger scales. The sound of bones popping and skin stretching echoed across the cavern. As the sound died away and the movement ceased, the great dragon was still.

Her once beautiful, silver scales were all blackened. Even though the fires burned her in her tiny elven form, the damage extended across the entire length of her true body.

And there she stayed.

The back half of her body blocked the exit tunnel in the back of the cave. Her great neck and head lay still on the floor of the cave with only slow, shallow puffs of dust to show she still breathed.

She tried to raise her head, but the best she could do was to open her eyes and stare at the wizard.

"If you do not take me soon," she said, "I fear that time shall rob you of your kill."

"There is time yet. There is the small matter of your eggs."

Kiranoth managed a tiny smile.

"There are none, wizard. My eggs have already gone to their bonded."

He frowned and narrowed his eyes. He started to say something to her but stopped and shook his head. He began chanting and moving his hands once more. Kiranoth tried to rise. Maybe she could blast him one more time if she could lift enough of her neck to draw a breath. But her body was too burnt and broken.

The elf finished casting his spell and tossed a small, orange ball to the ground. Without another word or a look back, the elf turned and strode from the cavern.

Kiranoth stared down at the tiny ball. It looked like such a harmless thing. But she knew it would be her death. She closed her eyes and waited. A little smile crept across her lips.

"Tarin," she said softly.

She drew a few more labored breaths before the ball exploded.

And then the Silver Queen was no more.

CHAPTER FOURTEEN

THE QUEEN IS DEAD

ELODY JOGGED BEHIND Eryninn and her brother trying hard to keep up as they made their way along the mountain trails. A large shadow danced on the ground in front of her, telling her that Jalthrax was keeping watch above. They weren't moving fast, but she was still struggling. Her sides ached from all the running, but she dared not ask the men to stop.

Her pace slowed as they reached the base of the mountain trail that would take them to the Silver Queen's cave. The path up the mountain to the entrance had never looked so long. She just managed to catch up to the others who were waiting before she fell to her knees. She sat there panting while the men looked up the mountain.

"Smoke," Eryninn said.

He pointed his hand up to the mouth of the cave. Elody sucked in her breath and looked up to where he was pointing. There was smoke drifting lazily out of cave. With a great effort she pulled herself to her feet.

"We have to go," she said. "Something is wrong."

"We don't know what's up there," her brother said.

"Can't be goblins," Eryninn said. "No way they'd come here. Even if they had brought an army with them, the dragon would destroy them."

Elody forced her shoulders back and stood straight.

"Something is wrong," she said again.

The men looked at her and then at each other. With a deep breath, Eryninn started first up the path to the cave. Despite her worries, Elody was glad he was moving cautiously. Even then she had trouble keeping up.

A shadow flew over her head, and she looked up to see Jalthrax flying toward the cave.

"No, Jalthrax!" she said.

The dragon didn't hear her and kept flying until he disappeared from sight. She started running. Her legs screamed in protest. She passed her brother and the half-elf who had already seen and were picking up their pace as well.

Elody ran for all she could.

Her legs and lungs were burning when she topped the path and stood in front of the cave. Her head throbbed. She was having trouble standing. She wanted to fall to the ground, but there was no time. She reached the top and saw the smoke floating out of the top of the cave, but she paid no attention as she charged in.

"Jalthrax!"

She heard the sounds of her brother and Eryninn catching up and pressed on into the cave. Once she was beyond the main entrance and into the large cavern, everything became clear.

Jalthrax was standing in the middle of the cave with his back to her. On the far side, a man in chain armor was kneeling. And in front of him was the charred remains of the Silver Queen.

The place reeked of burnt flesh and ash. The air was thick with the smell of smoke. What remained of the great dragon's body was still smoldering from the fires that had killed her. The sight of her made Elody gag.

She put her hand over her mouth to stifle a cry and block the stench, but it did no good. The smell and the pain were too much. She fell to her knees and vomited.

Then Rinn was there.

She could feel him kneel beside her and put his arm around her shoulders. The half-elf walked past both of them toward the man who was kneeling in front of the dragon's burnt corpse, and the man rose and turned at his approach. Elody immediately recognized Berym.

"Berym?" Elody said.

"Lady Elody," the knight said. "I had feared you and your brother dead."

Eryninn lowered his bow and walked past the knight without a word. He took a few slow steps and knelt down in front of the great dragon. Elody knelt quietly for a moment and watched as he lowered his head and placed a hand on her. He stroked her charred face and whispered gently, but Elody couldn't make out his words.

"What happened to her?" she asked.

"I do not know," Berym said. "I found her just as you see her now."

"How did you get here?" she asked. "Weren't you supposed to be protecting the village? Have you seen what those monsters did?"

Her sadness had given way to anger, and she could no longer control her voice as she began shouting.

"I stood beside the village as the goblin hordes poured in," Berym said. "I fought next to the men and boys of your village for as long as I could."

Rinn had moved up beside her and reached his hand for hers. She pulled her hand from his with a jerk, never turning to look at him.

"Then why are you here, alive, when they are all dead?" she yelled.

The knight sighed and hung his head. When at last he lifted it again, Elody could see the sadness in his eyes.

"The men and I, what remained of them after the initial attack, were trapped in the store. We had almost no warning that they were coming, but we were able to mount a defense. The men and I met them on the field just outside your farm. They poured out from the trees in a black and green wave."

The smoke in the cave was thickest near the body, and a bout of coughing overtook him. He grabbed up the water skin that hung at his belt and took a long drink.

"We fought them hard," he said. "Tried to give the women and children time to run. We killed many of them, but it seemed there were always more. A retreat was called, and we ran for the village. We regrouped and fled into the store when the goblins pressed us too hard to defend in the open. With our backs to the wall we defended it as our last refuge."

"How many were left?" Rinn asked.

"Only a dozen or so of the men after the first wave. We managed to fight them off for a while, but it was obvious to all who remained that none would make it out alive. The goblins lit the building on fire. As the smoke filled the room, Laren turned to me and told me to go and get help. He said to find the dragon and beg her to help them."

Berym coughed and took another drink of water.

"We formed a plan to rush the door. We knew the goblins would be waiting, so the men burst out in front with me in the rear. As the goblins stabbed and hacked at the men, I slashed my way through and escaped down the main road. I ran here to the cave as fast as I could. I had hoped that I could get here in time to enlist the dragon's aid to save the rest of the village. When I got here, this is what I found."

He swept his arm back toward the dead dragon as an explanation. Elody felt Jalthrax ease up behind her and put his head under her hand. She turned to look at him, but his eyes were low. He would not lift them to meet her gaze.

Eryninn rose quickly and moved to stand in front of the knight.

"Did you see anyone else here?" he asked.

"No one. The tracks I saw leading in were all old and too muddled to trace."

"Do you think goblins could have done this?" her brother asked.

"No," Eryninn said. "Goblins couldn't do this. It takes more than torches to burn the flesh of a dragon. It takes magical fire. *Strong* magic."

"Another dragonmage did this?" Rinn asked.

"No," Elody said firmly. "A dragonmage cannot wield power against a dragon. By the bond, the power we draw cannot harm another dragon."

"Then another dragon perhaps?" Berym asked.

Eryninn shook his head.

"She would not be caught in her cave with no escape. She'd have flown out and done battle in the air."

"A wizard," Elody said. "A wizard did this."

"A wizard," Eryninn said nodding. "A dragon hunter of old."

They looked at each other and all knew the implications. Wizards were rarely seen outside of elven lands since the great war between them and dragons. There were so few left now and were not to be trusted.

"What can we do now?" Elody asked. "We came here for her help."

"She would not have given it anyway," Eryninn said.

"Well we can't just do nothing!" Elody shouted.

Her brother tried to hold her hand again, but she only yanked it away and folded it into her robes. She stood with her arms crossed, glaring at Eryninn. He stared back, unblinking.

"We can fight," Berym said. "There are people down there in that village who may still be alive."

She could feel the tears welling up behind her eyes, but she wouldn't let them to fall. She didn't want to cry anymore. She felt like a child every time she cried in front of them. She turned away and faced Jalthrax.

The little dragon brought his head up to look her in the eyes. She fell to her knees and wrapped her arms around his neck.

"What can we do?" her brother asked. "There are only four of us."

"You can wait until the goblins crawl back to their holes and try to rescue any who are still alive," Eryninn said. "They might make camp right there in the square, but they might also up and leave now that they burned the place to the ground."

"They will stay," the knight said. "They were looting what little the villagers had from what I could see. They will stay and feast on their spoils until well into the night."

"Then maybe we have an advantage," Eryninn said. "We can't kill all of them, but maybe we can kill enough and sneak in to get the villagers out if any are still alive. How many do you think are down there?"

"I didn't get a good look with all of them running around, but there must be at least fifty of them left down there," Berym said. "Some were killed in the fight, and some were killed in the fire. I killed many myself before we became trapped."

"Most of them will be asleep if we go in at night," Eryninn said. "They'll be passed out full of drink and meat."

Elody was listening to the whole exchange, but through her tears, she watched Jalthrax. The little dragon was listening to the knight and the half-elf with intense focus. His head bobbed back and forth as each one spoke, and she could see him following their conversation. How much does he understand already?

"We should wait," Berym said. "I can send for other knights that might be in the area. They will come to our aid."

"There is no time," Eryninn said. "Whatever women are left down there are being tortured and raped. We have no time to find more help. We are it."

"I do not know you, sir, but I do not think the two of us can do this alone."

"Four of us," Rinn said.

"You are right," Eryninn said. "We'd never win in an all-out attack, but we have a chance to save the women."

"What of them?" Berym asked, cocking his head at Rinn and Elody.

Elody was still hugging Jalthrax's neck, and Rinn had knelt to put his arm around her. They both stood at the knight's mention of them.

"I may not be a knight, but I can kill goblins," Rinn said. "That is my home, and those are my people."

Elody rose quickly and pulled at Rinn's arm.

"I think we should go and get help," she said. "We can't go down there alone."

He turned back to look at her.

"There's no time, El. It has to be tonight. Everyone may be dead by morning."

"Everyone may be dead already, and we may be going to join them!"

"We have to try."

"No. We should get help. We can get more knights, like Berym said. We can ride to Buxbaum and bring back the militia."

"They won't come in time," Rinn said. "It has to be us."

"I've already lost Dad today," she whispered. "I can't lose you too."

She looked him the eyes, pleading with him. He stared back and put his hand on her arm.

"We have to help them, El."

"Why do you want to help them so badly? They *laughed* at you! They don't care about you!"

"Why do you *not* want to help them?"

"Why do you think I came here? The Silver Queen could have saved them, and she's dead! There's nothing *we* can do."

"There is no one else," Rinn said.

"Why are you risking your life for them? There's no one left to redeem yourself to!"

Rinn's jaw tightened, and he grabbed her arm.

"This is not about me," he said. "Those women need our help. They trained you to protect them."

"I don't owe them my life! I already gave them my father today, isn't that enough?"

He wrapped his arms around her and pulled her to him in a hug. Jalthrax pushed his head between them, and Elody's hand fell to his head. As she cried into Rinn's chest, he looked past her to the knight and the half-elf. He locked eyes with each of them.

"Will you come with us?" he asked.

"I will help rescue the women," Eryninn said. "Nothing more."

"I will help," Berym said.

Elody pulled away and wiped her cheek. She pulled her shoulders back and tried to stand and be brave.

"What can we do?" she asked.

"We will sneak in under cover of night and try to save anyone who is still alive," Eryninn said. "With enough stealth, we may all survive the night."

"Rinn can sneak in," the knight said, turning to Rinn.

"Me? Eryninn is much better at staying silent than I am."

"I am also more useful with a bow far removed from the battle. I can see at night as clear as if it were day. If there is trouble, you would not want me down in the thick of it where I am weaker."

"Remember your strengths, Rinn," Berym said. "Fight with your strengths."

Rinn looked back to Elody who was listening intently.

"No one can sneak through that village better than you," she said.

He looked back at the knight who was nodding. Rinn stood up straight and nodded. Berym clapped him on the back.

"We'll scout and find where they might be keeping prisoners and try to sneak in and get them out without arousing others," Eryninn said.

They all nodded.

Elody wrung her hands inside the folds of her robe and tried to steady her nerves. Jalthrax pressed his head against her. It calmed her, but she couldn't shake the feeling of dread inside of her. Then she felt Rinn close his hands over hers.

"We can do this," he said.

Elody hung her head.

"I'm not strong, Rinn."

"I'm not either. But *we* are."

She looked up into his eyes, and he gave her hands a tight squeeze. She nodded and managed a tiny smile.

"Let's get out of this cave," Eryninn called over his shoulder as he walked out. "We can rest and eat at the bottom of the mountain for a bit, but we need to reach the village before we lose the sun."

They all grabbed their things and ran to catch up.

CHAPTER FIFTEEN

VENGEANCE

ELODY CREPT CLOSELY behind the rest as they got near home. As the sun set over the burnt-out remains of the village, they got into place along the outskirts. They hid in the trees and watched as the goblins began their revelry. Camp fires were lit all around the village with one giant bonfire in the village square.

The goblins threw whatever wood they could find onto the bonfire. Elody watched as they tossed furniture and wood from the buildings around the square onto the fire. It roared high into the air as the goblins reveled in their spoils.

The goblins danced and laughed. They drank and cheered. From afar, it looked like just another village celebration.

But in the firelight, Elody could see the blood painted on their faces. Everywhere she looked, she saw the bodies. So many bodies. Stacked in piles, strewn between the campfires. Goblin and human alike.

But it was what the goblins *did* with the dead that

made Elody sick. The goblins drank the blood of their enemies. They painted their bodies in it. They gave praise to their horrible Blood God, shouting his name to the heavens.

Eryninn and Berym both stood stiff and unmoving. Their faces were like stone. Elody walked over to stand next to them and felt Eryninn tense beside her. His face was hard, and his jaw was tight.

"We wait," Eryninn said. "Let them have their fun. None of them will live to see the dawn."

"That wasn't part of the plan," Berym said as he moved to stand in front of the half-elf. "The plan was to rescue anyone alive and get out. We can't kill fifty goblins in a fight."

Berym tried to keep his voice a whisper, but Elody could still hear him clearly. She glanced back at the village, but none of the goblins seemed to hear them.

"They set no watch," Eryninn said. "They aren't expecting a fight tonight, and that means they aren't expecting us."

"The plan was for Rinn to sneak in and try and rescue some of the women and children if there are any left alive. That was it. We cannot fight an entire goblin army."

"That is not an army. They are more than a tribe, but it is *not* an army. There are fewer than I imagined."

"There are more than we can take in a fight," Berym said. "If we go charging into that village, swords waving, not a one of us will come back out."

"I thought you were ready for a fight," Eryninn said.

"I thought you wanted to avoid one," Berym said.

Rinn stepped between the two of them and looked Eryninn in the eye.

"I thought this wasn't your fight," he said.

"I made it my fight," Eryninn said.

"Why?"

"My reasons are my own. Do you want to kill these goblins or not?"

Rinn eyed him curiously for a long time and then turned back to Berym. He drew his dagger and gripped it in his hand.

"We kill them all, or we die trying," Rinn said.

The knight shook his head.

"You would lead your sister to her death for vengeance? Vengeance will only add more bodies to their fires. It will not bring anyone back."

"Elody will rescue the women and children," Rinn said. "Once we start fighting, any goblins there will rush to join the fight, leaving them unprotected. She can sneak them out into the woods."

"Even drunk and bloated we cannot take fifty goblins or more," the knight said. "Many of them will die, but we will surely die with them."

"What if some of them aren't up to fight?" Rinn said. "I can sneak through their sleeping lines and slit their throats before many of them can wake for battle. Most of them will be so drunk they won't even know I'm there. If I can kill even a dozen of them or more before the fighting starts, we can take them all."

"I might be able to help," Elody said. "I have spells."

Eryninn looked up at Berym. The knight stared back

at him and then looked at Elody and Rinn.

"We don't have to kill them all," Eryninn said. "If we kill enough and cause a panic, they will run. Goblins are fast creatures, and never faster than when they are running for their own lives."

Berym just kept shaking his head and sighing.

"This is folly," he said. "She is a child, and he is barely a man!"

"I became the only man in my family when the goblins killed my father this morning," Rinn said.

Berym stared at each of them in turn before his shoulders slumped in defeat.

"Very well," he said. "If that is your wish, then I will fight with you. We will go in a few hours when they are all drunk. I'd rather be facing drunk goblins if it's all the same to you."

"I'd rather be facing dead goblins," Eryninn said.

***

They waited several hours more for the goblins to drink themselves into a stupor. Elody had taken Jalthrax farther away from the village to keep him quiet. He hadn't opened his mouth much since they found his mother in the cave, but she couldn't keep him still.

Elody sat on the ground, and Jalthrax laid down beside her and rested his head in her lap. She absentmindedly stroked his neck as she thought about her part in the coming fight.

She wanted to fight alongside her brother and their brave new friends. She wanted to help them. But there was a chance they would all fall and no one would be left to save the villagers. Elody made a silent vow to herself that once everyone was safe in the woods she would turn back to help fight.

After a time she heard someone coming through the woods. Jalthrax lifted his head from her lap, and she stood quickly as Rinn approached. He waved his hand for her to follow.

"It's time," he said. "The fires burn low, and the goblins are all too drunk to stoke them."

She nodded and dusted her robes off as she and Jalthrax fell into step behind him. Her brother made no attempt to keep his steps quiet, so she didn't bother either. They hurried back to Eryninn and Berym who were still waiting where she had left them.

"Okay," Eryninn said, "Rinn goes in first and sneaks through the camp killing anyone sleeping or too drunk to stand. Elody moves around to the far side of the village where the women are being kept and waits for the fighting to start."

"If we hear or see a commotion," Berym said, "I will shout a charge and run down the main street toward the square. If Rinn is caught, he will need the distraction to draw any attention away from him and onto me. If Rinn does his job without detection, he'll meet back up with us on the north road, and we'll all sneak in quickly."

They all nodded together. Rinn stepped toward Elody and wrapped his arms around her.

"Be safe," he said. "I love you."

He drew his dagger from his belt and gripped it tightly in his hand. With a final look back, he disappeared into the darkness toward the village.

"That's your cue," Eryninn said.

Elody nodded. She looked back at Jalthrax who was standing ready behind her and set off around the outside of the village. She was headed in the opposite direction from Eryninn when he turned and grabbed her by the arm. She turned back to look at him and saw the hardened look in his eyes.

"Don't be afraid to use your power, Elody," the half-elf said. "These goblins don't deserve your mercy."

Elody could only nod.

Eryninn let her arm go and snuck down past the outer farms toward the village. She watched him for a second before he disappeared into the darkness, and she could see him no more. She turned and made her way through the trees and around the burnt houses and buildings.

Elody made it around to the south side of the village easily enough. To where Eryninn had scouted the women earlier. The goblins were keeping some of the women alive, trapped inside a burned out building.

She could see a fire still burning brightly in the remains of the building. Some goblins were still awake and moving around. Just outside the firelight she could see several women huddling against the remains of the walls. Women she knew. She heard muffled cries from the building and could see the ugly back and head of a goblin on top of one of the women.

Elody closed her eyes and steadied herself. She wanted to leap from her cover and blast the thing out of existence, but she stayed her hand. Their whole plan hinged on stealth. And a lot of luck. She forced herself to watch as the goblin continued his frantic pace. She could hear every cry and sob, and she knew then that she would not hesitate to burn these goblins to ash.

Her eyes were so fixed on the terrible scene in front of her that by the time she heard the footsteps behind her they were already too close.

***

Eryninn crept through the darkness past one of the outer farms that was still mostly intact. He stopped and listened at a window for a second, but hearing nothing, he moved on. Through the night, he made his way to the few buildings that remained just outside the village square.

When he reached the town, he squeezed between two burned out buildings and slid along the alleyway toward the main street. There were goblins all around him, but he didn't pause for a moment. He crept through the darkness and took in his surroundings.

The goblins, what few remained standing, were all shouting and singing in their native tongue. And they were all still drinking heavily. Most were drunk and stumbling about. A few were already passed out in the streets. The ones that were still up and partying just stepped over the prone ones, never bothering to stop their revelry.

When Eryninn reached the smithy near the village square, he found most of it still intact. The building was made of stone and had survived the initial firebombing.

Glancing quickly down both sides of the alley, he stuck his fingers in the crevices between the stones and pulled himself quietly and skillfully up the wall.

Once he reached the top, Eryninn swung his leg up and over and pulled himself onto the roof. He laid flat and crawled carefully to the edge where he could watch.

When the fighting started, he would be ready.

***

Rinn crept cautiously toward the village. There were almost no goblins on the north side of the village, so it was clear all the way to the bonfire in the square. The fire had burned low leaving a mountain of coals radiating heat. It left the square bathed in a glowing, orange darkness.

Rinn held the dagger tight in his hand and crept along outside of the firelight until he reached the first building. He leaned his back against the only remaining wall and waited there. His heart pounded in his ears.

He looked over and saw his shadow dance along the wall of the building and backed deeper into the alley. He was used to sneaking through the village in total darkness, and many of his favorite dark corners were now lit by the fires. He would have to be more careful.

With a glance around the corner, Rinn crept to the back of the building and slid through the shadows until he was behind the old general store. The entire thing had been burned to the ground, but there was enough rubble for him to duck down and hide.

So far so good.

Other than a few drunken shouts, he'd heard no

voices and seen very little movement. The goblins were mostly either sleeping or passed out. As he peered over the remains of the wall, he still didn't spot any goblins. Rinn stood to slip past when he heard a grumble and glanced down to see a goblin sleeping just on the other side of his wall.

He ducked back down and silently cursed himself. Crouching low and feeling the weight of the dagger in his hand, he said a silent prayer before slowly standing back up. He peered over the wall and let out a silent sigh when he saw the goblin still sleeping soundly.

What remained of the wall was short enough that he could easily reach his arm over it. He stood there staring at the sleeping goblin for another second.

Do it.

Rinn took a deep breath and steeled his nerves. Then he plunged the dagger down into the goblin's throat.

Its eyes burst open in a panic as its breath was suddenly cut off. Arms flapping wildly, it grabbed at the knife and tried to pull it out, but it had no strength. After a bit more struggling, the hands fell away and dropped to the ground.

Rinn gave the knife a twist and then jerked it from the corpse. He stooped to wipe the blood on the goblin's body before crouching back behind the wall and moving deeper into what remained of his village.

Once he got past the square he could see more goblins. Most of them were laid out on the ground. Some of them had made it to a campfire or a bedroll before passing out, but most had simply dropped where they stood and fallen asleep in the middle of the street.

Rinn made his way cautiously through the village and toward any prone goblin he could see. The ones passed out in the street were the easiest. They smelt heavily of drink, and he knew they wouldn't struggle.

At each one he found, he stopped and drove his dagger through its neck. Some of them struggled. Some didn't even move as their life left them. A few were passed out on their stomachs, and he would press his knee into their back as he struck to keep the struggling down.

With each kill, his hand became steadier and more sure. The window of hesitation before taking a life was shrinking. He counted over half a dozen now that lay dead by his blade. He heard sounds of someone coming and ducked back into the shadows. A goblin came into view as he stumbled down the street toward the bonfire.

Rinn froze as the goblin walked past the still-bleeding one he'd just stabbed. Just keep walking. If the goblin stopped to check its companion, they were caught. Je held his breath for several seconds as the goblin passed by. He relaxed once it was out of sight.

With renewed caution, Rinn crept back out into the street.

***

Berym sat quietly in the darkness. He couldn't see anything that was going on beyond the firelight, but he remained calm. He was used to the long, still wait before a battle. When the fighting began, he would be ready.

He had moved closer to the village, but he was still

within the tree line. None of the goblins were even keeping a watch for a potential attack, but he kept his sword near him and sat ready to move when the alarm was sounded. Which he hoped would be a while. The longer things were silent, the better chance they all had of seeing the dawn.

Berym worried about Rinn. Elody was far enough out of the battle that she would probably be safe if she got away with the women. But Rinn was down there in the middle of them all.

He squinted at the darkness, trying to catch some glimpse or hint of Rinn's position, but he saw nothing. Good. If he could see Rinn, so could the goblins.

Berym drew his sword and stared down the length of its blade. The steel was polished to a flawless shine. The edge perilously sharp. He tilted the blade back and forth and watched the moonlight dance across the etchings along the blade.

"Watch over me, old friend. I'm not ready to see you again just yet."

Berym gave the blade one more twist before dropping it back into its sheathe.

***

Rinn continued his hunt through the village, murdering every goblin in his path. He had met no resistance so far. Some were so drunk that they died with nothing but a gurgle as their blood spilled out.

A few goblins stumbled through the village, and Rinn had to duck back into the shadows a few times. None of the conscious ones had noticed anything amiss and sounded the alarm. Rinn said a silent prayer of thanks for that.

As he moved deeper into the village, he saw a bright fire still glowing in the charred remains of a building. Several goblins were still up and moving around, so he stopped and watched them from the shadows. He caught sight of some movement and turned to look out past the fire where he saw a glint of metal.

Elody and Jalthrax were hiding in some trees just outside that building. They were out in the open where he could see them. Rinn tried to think of some way to signal them that she could be seen, but he could find no easy way without alerting the goblins as well. He could only hope that no one would see her there.

He surveyed the rest of the goblins he could see. Most of them were sleeping around the remaining fires in clusters, and he could see no easy way to get to them without putting himself in the middle of them all. He started to wonder how he could separate some of them when he saw more movement near Elody.

***

Elody spun around with a spell on her lips, but she knew already that she was too late. She swung her hands in wide circles trying to get off a spell but then stopped suddenly as a young boy appeared from behind a tree.

"Elody?" he whispered.

Elody quickly dismissed her spell and felt the magic fade from her fingers. It was a young boy, about eight, coming at her through the darkness.

"Drey?" she said.

The little boy smiled and rushed to hug her. She grabbed him and pulled him close to her. He started crying, and Elody pulled him tight into her robes to muffle the cries. She shot a look back over her shoulder and was relieved to see that no one had noticed them.

"What are you doing out here?" she said.

She waited a minute for the boy to catch his breath and stop crying long enough to explain.

"When the goblins attacked, my mom gathered us and the rest of the children and sent us off into the woods to hide. We've been hiding out here waiting for them to go away. When are they going to go away, Elody?"

He started crying again. She rocked him gently and tried to shush him.

"Where are the others? Are there any of the older kids with you?"

"No," he said, wiping his eyes. "The older boys stayed to fight."

"What about the girls? The older girls. Are they with you?"

"They took them. They took them all and, and…"

He cried again. Elody pulled him to her and hugged him.

"Listen," she whispered. "I need you to go back into the woods and wait for me with the others."

"No! Don't leave!"

Elody put a finger over his mouth and shushed him.

"I need to go and get your mom and the others out. I need you to go back and protect the little ones. Can you do that for me?"

He nodded and wiped the tears from his eyes.

"You have to watch over them, Drey."

"I'll keep them safe," he said. "When will you come and find us?"

"Soon," Elody said. "As soon as I get your mom and the others to safety, we'll all come find you in the woods. I need you to take the little ones and stay hidden so that no one can find you until you hear us call for you. Do you understand?"

"Yes."

"Good boy. Now go."

He ran back into the woods.

Elody turned back to the women. No more. I have to do something. She couldn't kill every goblin on her own, but maybe she could stop *these* goblins.

Without even a glance at Jalthrax, she reached her hand out to him and felt the magic flow into her instantly. She took a deep breath and started moving. Her hands flicked through the air, weaving the threads of magic into a spell. Elody closed her eyes as she fell into the rhythm.

For his part, Jalthrax stood perfectly still when she began casting. She could feel him beside her, but he didn't move a muscle once her fingers started moving. As if he sensed her concentration and his role.

She opened her eyes and focused her thoughts on the two goblins who walked around the women. The ones guarding them. As her hands finished their dance, she pointed a finger at the two of them and felt the magic leave her body in a rush.

The two goblins both stopped moving in an instant. They just stood there, swaying slightly in the night air.

Elody held her breath and waited. She had only cast this particular spell a few times and never without her amulet. Several seconds went by with no movement. Her whole body tensed. She crouched down ready to run. And then, to her great relief, the goblins slowly lowered themselves to the ground.

In another moment they were snoring loudly. Elody pulled herself up proudly and smiled. It worked perfectly. There were no other goblins in the house, and the women were safe for now.

Now I have to save them.

Elody crept through the darkness toward the house and came to the back wall. When one of the girls in the house saw her she pulled her legs tight to her and huddled against the wall. Elody put her finger to her lips and then waved for her to come.

Peeking her head over her knees, a look of recognition came over her when she looked at Elody. She glanced nervously around at the sleeping goblins in the house. Elody looked at them too and heard them snoring loudly. She waved her hand again for the girl to come.

The other women in the house watched this exchange and were now moving quietly to where Elody stood. One by one they went over the remains of the wall. Elody put her fingers to her lips again, motioning for them to remain silent. Once all the girls were safely over, Elody waved for them to follow her. She moved slowly with

Jalthrax beside her and crept back to the safety of the forest.

They had almost made it to the trees when they heard a scream.

***

Rinn saw the goblin walking toward the house where the girls were being kept. He shot a glance at Elody, but she wasn't looking up. She was standing at the back of the building and waving to the girls. She didn't see it coming.

Rinn had only a second to act.

The goblin was stumbling drunk, but even *it* would notice the girls escaping. Rinn stepped out of the shadows and fell in behind it. He timed his step, hoping he could make the kill clean and quiet.

The goblin looked up at the house, and Rinn saw its body suddenly stiffen. Rinn stepped closer and stabbed his dagger into the goblin's back. He had hoped to pierce a lung or something that would prevent it from crying out, but he was not that skillful yet.

The goblin gave a panicked yell before sliding off his dagger and falling to the ground. Rinn went into a crouch and looked around hoping no one had heard the yell. No such luck. Goblins all around him were stirring from their sleep and grabbing at their weapons.

Not knowing what else to do, Rinn dove over the wall of the nearest building and into the midst of the sleeping goblins his sister had knocked out. Staying low to the ground and hidden by the remnants of the walls, he crept to the two sleeping goblins and slit their throats.

Two more down.

***

Berym heard the cry cut through the night and leapt to his feet.

Drawing his sword, he charged down the main road as fast as he could move. If the alarm had already been sounded there was no need for stealth. His job now was to try and distract some of the goblins and draw them toward him so that Elody and Rinn would be safe.

At a hard run, Berym reached the village square in half a minute. He caught sight of movement somewhere overhead and glanced up to see Eryninn stand and draw his bow from one of the remaining rooftops. Berym said a silent prayer and charged in.

One goblin who had been sleeping nearest the fire had pulled himself to his knees at the sound of the alarm and was now looking for his weapon. Berym charged, hoping to end it quickly. Before he could reach it, an arrow thunked into his chest and laid it down again.

Berym skipped past and met another goblin who was coming around the other side of the fire. It brought its sword up for a feeble swing, but Berym easily batted it away and ran it through. He yanked his blade from the dying creature and came around the other side of the fire.

The goblins had not yet organized any kind of resistance, but several were up and ready to fight. Three of them rushed the knight hoping to catch him off guard.

But Berym had been waiting all night for this.

He pulled up his shield to block the oncoming attacks and then waded in with his sword. An arrow flew over his shoulder and laid one of the goblins low. The other two squealed and scrambled back as their companion fell, but Berym charged after them.

The knight kicked the closest goblin, knocking it back a few feet, and then thrust his sword at the other. The creature squealed and jumped, just managing to get its own sword up to block.

The goblin parried the blow and Berym pressed the attack harder. The one that had been kicked to the ground stood up and joined the fight. A twang from Eryninn's bow put an arrow through its eye.

The remaining goblin shrieked and jumped back as the knight swung again. Then it turned and ran. Berym charged after it, but the nimble goblin was much faster than the heavily armored knight.

More goblins were rushing to meet him.

A soft twang over his shoulder, and one of them fell screaming to the ground. The rest of the small group held back as it thrashed around. Berym was still chasing the one running away from him. It burst through the others, spinning them around, and kept on running.

They turned back to see a mass of armor pressing down on them.

***

Elody made sure the women helped each other as they ran. A few of them were injured, but most of their pain was not physical. Several of them had to stop to help others up and keep them moving. Once they were deeper into the forest, Elody turned back to the village.

"Go!" she shouted. "The children are hiding in the forest. Go and find them and then stay hidden. We will come to you when the fighting is over."

The women looked confused, but no one was going to argue about sticking around. They all ran as fast as they could. Elody whispered a prayer for them and then headed back for the village.

With Jalthrax behind her, Elody didn't even stop to be silent. There was no need for stealth anymore. She quickly made it back to the house and went around the outside trying to sneak toward the square. She could see Berym fighting against a group of goblins and moved to join him when a hand closed over her arm and yanked her down.

She stifled a scream as she hit the ground and tried to yank her arm back.

"Shhh!"

Elody opened her eyes and saw Rinn laying low to the ground.

"Stay down," he said. "We'll do better if we stay out of sight and find small fights where we can."

She nodded her head and looked up at Jalthrax who was staring off into the darkness with his neck held high.

"We're not going to hide very well with him," she said.

"Let's just hope the sight of even a *baby* dragon will be enough to keep them from coming over."

Rinn crawled across the floor to the doorway and peered out. Elody followed behind him with Jalthrax coming around the outside of the building. She saw a goblin running down the street with Berym chasing after it. And they were coming this way.

"Stay down," her brother said.

Berym gave up the chase when a larger group of goblins came up the street, but the running goblin burst through and kept on running. When it got near enough to the house, Rinn jumped out of hiding and onto its back. It yelled in surprise as they both tumbled to the ground. They rolled a few times, and Rinn managed to pin the creature down. Grabbing his dagger, he jabbed down and stabbed it through the chest. The goblin screamed and thrashed and grabbed at his arms before its hands went slack and then fell to the dirt.

Rinn yanked his dagger free and stood. Elody looked back up the street to see Berym facing off against a half dozen goblins. She heard several twangs somewhere near the square and felt some relief as she saw two of the goblins fall. She looked around the campsites and saw a group of four more that were forming a small line and moving in behind the four that were still facing the knight.

She shook Rinn's shoulder and pointed at the smaller group.

"I see them," he said. "What do we do? Can you put them all to sleep?"

"Not this time," she said. "I need you to distract them. Get them to turn around and come back this way."

"Hey! Woo!"

Rinn picked up a rock and threw it at the four goblins

sneaking in behind their companions. They all turned as one and saw them. A boy, a girl and a baby dragon. They looked back at the tall man in gleaming armor and the deadly arrows that were dropping their kin like flies and must have decided they liked these odds better.

Elody began casting as soon as they turned. They saw that Rinn held nothing but a dagger, and the dragon was standing perfectly still. They wasted no time in closing the distance.

Through the haze of her magic she could feel her brother tense next to her, but he said nothing. She knew he was trying not to break her concentration. She could feel the power from Jalthrax and felt his presence on her other side.

The four goblins closed on them, weapons drawn.

"Elody," she heard her brother say.

With a final flick of her wrist, Elody slashed her hand across her body in an arc. As her fingers traced through the darkness, a fan of flames spread out from her fingertips and engulfed the approaching goblins.

They all screamed. They fell to the ground and writhed in agony. Elody smelled the foul stench of burning flesh. But she would not look away. She watched it all, never taking her eyes from them.

She felt no pity for the goblins as they burned.

***

Eryninn loosed another arrow into a goblin on the knight's left side, dropping him. Berym was breathing a little harder, but he was still standing strong. Amazing. In all that heavy armor, he should be too tired to even stand. Even at this distance, Eryninn could see dark blood splashed over the knight's shield and armor, but he looked otherwise unscathed.

The goblins were on the run now.

What few remained had grabbed whatever they could carry and charged for the trees. Eryninn loosed a few more shots at their retreating backs before jumping from the roof and landing lightly with a roll. He came up and took a few quick steps to stand beside Berym. The two of them stood and watched them go, neither making a move to stop them.

"We shall have to go on a hunt tomorrow," Eryninn said.

"Maybe the day after tomorrow," Berym said. "I'm beat."

The knight smiled down at the half-elf and then followed his gaze. They had both seen the flash of fire as Elody's spell went off. They saw her standing with Rinn and Jalthrax in front of four charred goblins and walked over to meet them.

Eryninn looked down to the four smoldering goblins and then back up to Elody. She picked her head up and stared him down. Were it not for the corpses around her, her look would be that of any other stubborn teenager. He turned away to hide the pained look on his face.

"They're on the run," Berym said as he got nearer.

"Should we go after them?" Rinn asked.

"No. Let them run. We'll track them down another time. There has been enough blood spilled tonight."

Eryninn looked down at the four dead goblins and

back up at Elody again. She had her hand on Jalthrax's head and was stroking it as she looked into the darkness at the fleeing goblins. Her fingers tensed, and he waited for her to meet his eyes.

"We've done enough," he said as she looked at him. "There might be wounded to tend to, and we need to fetch the women and children from the woods. No more fighting this night."

Eryninn held her gaze as he spoke and waited for her to respond. She watched the fleeing goblins but then turned back to the forest where the women had run. She nodded. Her face softened a little and her shoulders fell. The half-elf nodded to himself as much to her and then marched off into the forest to find the women and children.

CHAPTER SIXTEEN

LEAVING JORNATH

ELODY WOKE WITH a start.

She heard voices around her and sat up quickly. She sat on a soft bedroll, but she couldn't remember how she had gotten there. Some of the women from the village were walking around a fire, and she wondered for a moment if she had dreamed the whole thing.

As she took in her surroundings she knew it had not been a dream. They were all in the village square. She could see the buildings all around her that had been destroyed by the fires. The goblins had burned all but a few structures to the ground.

Some of the women stared unblinking at the fire. Some sat and wept softly into their hands. Many still were up and working, preparing food. Elody marveled at their strength. Some of them had just lost their husbands, their children, everything in this world, and still they woke with the dawn to do what needed to be done.

"You fell asleep so suddenly I was worried for you,"

Rinn said.

She turned to see him sitting on a bedroll next to hers and petting Jalthrax. The sight made her smile.

"He likes you," she said.

"Nah. He's just too tired to get up. He's not so bad though. Just a big lizard, really."

Jalthrax raised his head and snorted, blowing Rinn's hair back.

"Ahh, that's cold!"

"Careful, brother. He understands more than you think."

Her brother only smiled and continued to rub the dragon's neck. Jalthrax laid his head back down next to Rinn and closed his eyes.

"The magic takes a lot out of you, doesn't it? We made camp around the big fire, and you laid down and fell asleep like you hadn't slept in weeks. Even Jalthrax hasn't stirred much this morning."

"It was a hard day for everyone," she said as she looked down at the ground.

Elody could feel the tears welling up in her eyes again.

No. No more tears.

She breathed slowly and forced them away. She picked her head up and panned around the square, looking at all of the faces. A hard day for everyone. Elody looked for Eryninn and spotted him standing off in the distance.

"He's keeping watch in case any goblins return," Rinn said.

"Does he think they'll come back?"

"No, but he doesn't want to take any chances. He says none of the women are strong enough to fight if they come back, so he doesn't want to be caught off guard."

Elody looked around at them all and thought the half-elf just might be wrong about the strength of these women. She scanned the faces and then looked at Rinn who was still looking down.

"Fawn?" she asked.

He shook his head and kept rubbing Jalthrax's neck.

"I'm sorry, Rinn."

He nodded.

She watched him, waiting for him to look up at her, but he wouldn't. Elody looked around again, trying to spot Berym. She strained her neck looking, but she didn't see him anywhere.

"Where is Berym?"

Rinn cleared his throat.

"He took a horse and rode off for Buxbaum at dawn. He won't return until tomorrow morning at the earliest."

"What time is it?"

"Nearly midday."

Elody blinked.

Have I been asleep that long? The magic must have taken more out of her than she realized. She had used more magic yesterday than she had ever attempted in her training. She looked down at Jalthrax who was enjoying his rubdown and wondered if he felt the same sort of drain from giving her his power.

"Well," she said, "I guess I'd better help with the

food."

She stood up and felt lightheaded. She steadied herself before trying to walk, and the feeling went away. She straightened her shoulders and brushed the dust off of her robes and then went to help the other girls.

**

It was nearly midday on the following day when Berym returned. He rode his horse into the village with a small caravan of people following behind him. Several men dressed in armor rode in a small wagon being pulled by oxen.

When they reached the square, Berym dismounted and walked over to the gathering that was forming. The rest of the men got down from the carts and stood behind him in a group.

"These good men are here to help us all," Berym said. "They have brought food and supplies and hands to help rebuild. We will start work in the morning. I have sent word to the knighthood for more to come and defend in case of further attacks. Your neighbors have graciously loaned us some of their militia who will stay and help protect you all as well."

He waved his hands at some of the men behind him who all stood up straight. Elody recognized Arina as she stepped forward to speak for the women. She was the only remaining elder of the village. She had lost her husband in the Kingdom Wars many years ago. Now she had lost her only son.

"Thank you all for coming," she said. "It means so much that you would all come this far to help us. But there is nothing here to rebuild."

"But there is *much* to rebuild," Berym said. "Do not let the goblins take your homes from you after everything else they have taken."

Arina closed her eyes and took a deep breath. When she opened them again, Elody could see the strength of resolve in her eyes.

"We have no homes here, good knight. These are walls of wood and stone. A home is where our families lived, where our husbands lived... Where our chil-"

She choked up and couldn't continue.

Mara stepped forward and put her arms around Arina's waist. She took a breath and shook her head as if to shake the tears from her heart. She wiped them from her face and looked the knight in the eyes.

"We have no homes here," Arina said. "We could rebuild, but with no men, and so far from anywhere, we would not survive for long, I fear. We humbly thank you all for your offer, but you have your own families who need you. We could not ask you to stay and protect us here so far from your homes."

Berym could only nod.

"Then we shall see you to where you would go," the knight said. "These good men will travel home with the dawn if no one is to stay. I have been offered a wagon and supplies to take you all to Havnor or anywhere in between if that is where you wish to go."

"We will discuss it amongst ourselves," Arina said.

They turned to form a circle and talked softly. Berym gave his horse a pat on the neck and then walked over to

Elody and Rinn.

"I will take you both to Havnor, to your aunt, if you like."

"We're not leaving our home," Rinn said.

"You heard the woman," Berym said. "There is no home here."

"I will not leave my father's farm to the goblins or whoever else would come to take it," Rinn said.

"There will be no one here," Berym said. "You wish to live on the frontier, days from the rest of the world, with no help? No one to trade with? Buxbaum is the closest town, more than a day away on horseback, and it is no bigger than here. This is no place for a young man and his younger sister to live alone."

Elody looked at her brother.

"This is our chance, Rinn," she said. "You told me that you wanted to leave, but you couldn't. Now you can. We can both leave."

He looked at her, and she could see the pain written across his face.

"Think of your sister, Rinn. She's still a young girl. She cannot live out here, just the two of you. Think of yourself. You are old enough to find a wife and start your own family. You will not do those things here. Not anymore."

Rinn looked at her, and she saw his shoulders slump. He hung his head in defeat and nodded. Berym reached out and clasped Rinn by the arm. He looked into the knight's eyes and nodded again.

Arina called to the knight as their circle broke apart.

"We will go to Buxbaum," she said. "Havnor is too long a journey, and we are too beaten. Perhaps we may return to Jornath with some new families when the ground thaws. Maybe then we can begin to rebuild."

Berym nodded.

"These men will take you as soon as you are ready to travel," he said. "I will take Elody and Rinn to Havnor with me. I shall pray for a good journey for all."

He turned back to Elody and Rinn.

"Gather your things. We'll leave in the morning."

***

Elody woke with the sun and began packing for their journey. She and Rinn collected whatever meager belongings they could find on the farm that had not burned up and then went back to the square to find Berym. They found him talking to Eryninn near the fire. The rest of the women from the village had already piled into a wagon and left for Buxbaum, leaving only the four of them and Jalthrax.

Eryninn had organized some of the men to build a giant pyre outside the village where they stacked and burned the bodies of the goblins. They tried to bury all the men and women they found, but it was too big a job for a small crew. They settled on a second pyre where they could burn the bodies of the villagers separately from the goblins.

Elody looked around her at the destruction.

She could still see where the ground was soaked with blood, and the smoke was heavy in the air from the fires and the burning bodies. She turned her head back to her father's farm and felt the tears sting her eyes once more. She wiped them away with the sleeve of her robe and turned to listen to Eryninn and Berym.

"I'll come as far as the Witch's Cross, and then I'm on my way back home," Eryninn said.

"And I shall appreciate the company that far. Perhaps one day you'll come and visit us all in Havnor."

"Are you going to stay there a while?"

"If I can," he said and looked back to Elody and Rinn. "Long enough to help them settle in. You'll come and visit then?"

"I just might," Eryninn said. "Perhaps I'll track down where these goblins came from. They're on the run now, but a force that large won't run for long."

He smiled at the knight and extended his arm. Berym grasped it firmly, and they held for several seconds before letting go.

Berym turned and mounted his horse, signaling for everyone to make ready. Rinn climbed into the driver's seat of the wagon with all of their belongings in the back. Eryninn climbed into the back of the wagon and then held his hand down to pull Elody up. She didn't need the help, but she smiled and took it anyway.

Rinn gave a snap of the reins, and the wagon lurched down the road. Jalthrax gave a screech and leapt into the air. He flew above them in ever-widening circles as they rode. Elody crept up front to sit on the buckboard next to Rinn. He smiled and ruffled his hand through her hair, which she promptly slapped away.

They rode in silence for several minutes before one of

them spoke.

"So what do we do now?" Rinn asked.

Elody looked down and watched the ground passing beneath her feet.

"I want to find who killed the Silver Queen," she said at last.

"Why?"

"She is a dragon mother. Jalthrax's mother. Someone should find out who did it."

"Does it have to be you?"

"No, but I can't just let it go like nothing happened. Someone should avenge her death."

"I don't know, El. It'd take a powerful dragonmage to find a wizard like that," he said.

She sighed.

"Then I'll have to become a powerful dragonmage," she said.

Rinn looked down at her and smiled, but she was staring off into the distance. Above them, Jalthrax screeched and flew out ahead toward the mountains.

"Where's he off to?" Rinn asked.

"I don't know," Elody said. "Maybe to say goodbye to his mother?"

"Should we wait for him?"

"No."

"How will he find us down the road?" Rinn said.

Elody watched as Jalthrax disappeared into the distant peaks.

"He'll always find me," she said.

CHAPTER SEVENTEEN

CHAMPION OF OGROSH

GORTOGH WAS NEVER meant to lead a goblin tribe. But now he found himself the chief of the largest goblin tribe the once powerful kingdom of Essrel had ever seen. And what he saw before him now had him shaking in anger. Goblins, all members of his tribe, limping back into camp with life-threatening wounds and dragging the dead behind them.

The remnants of a force he had sent to a small village in the south, now all but destroyed.

Gortogh clenched and unclenched his fists trying to control his anger as he looked for someone to explain. He found only one of the hunting party leaders he had assigned still alive. The pathetic goblin was barking orders at the remainder of the force from the back of the group.

Gortogh stalked through the camp toward him. Some goblins bowed at his feet as he passed while others scrambled quickly away from his wrath. His anger flowed off of him in waves that made them all shiver in fear.

"Bograr!" Gortogh shouted.

The hunting party leader stopped yelling and looked up at the approach of his chief. His expression turned cold. He held up his hands and backed away as he tried to speak.

"It was dragon, Mighty Chief! Dragon and a girl who commanded it! They attack and kill us all!"

"You not hurt!" Gortogh yelled as he continued to stalk the frightened goblin.

"Me had to run to save others! Girl and dragon threw fire that burned us up! And knights and elves! A whole army attack us!"

Gortogh growled and strode faster. Bograr backed over a tree root and tripped. He stumbled back a few steps before catching his feet and then turned in an all-out run. Gortogh made no move to hurry after him as he drew his longsword.

The little goblin was running as fast as he could now. He looked back to see the chief with his sword drawn and thanked Ogrosh he had not drawn a bow. Bograr looked over his shoulder and called out as he ran.

"It not my fault! It was elves and knights! It was girl and dragon! They shoot powerful fire! It not my fault!"

"You are leader!" Gortogh yelled. "It always your fault!"

He pointed the tip of his sword at the back of the fleeing goblin and loosed its magic. He wasn't even sure how to do it, but he felt something tingle in the hilt. It was his first time to use the power of the sword. He wanted the rest of the tribe to see his might and see clearly the price of failure. A blue crackle of energy flowed from the hilt and down the blade before leaping from the tip as a great bolt of lightning.

The lightning flew unerringly towards its target. Bograr turned his head to see what the loud noise he heard was, but he never saw it coming. The bolt struck him hard in the back. All of his muscles tensed as the energy wracked his helpless body. The force of it lifted him from the ground and hurled him through the air like a doll before slamming him into a tree with a sickening crunch. His body fell to the ground with a lifeless thud. Gortogh turned back to face the assembled tribe.

"I am the will of Ogrosh!"

He stalked through the gathered throng and back to his cave without another word. The other goblins cowered and groveled in subjugation before his feet as he moved through them. And Gortogh loved every minute of it.

He reached the cave and found Velanon waiting.

"The power feels good, yes?"

"I grow tired of these visits, wizard. I am in a foul mood today."

"Has something happened to put you in this mood?"

"I lost more than fifty warriors raiding that village!"

"Is that all?" Velanon asked casually. "I had expected twice that many."

"You don't even care?" Gortogh shouted. "You don't care that I lost nearly a third of the warriors under my command?"

Gortogh was yelling now. He caught himself and tried to lower his voice. He didn't want the others to enter and see him talking to an elf.

"No, I don't," Velanon said.

"You don't care about failure?"

"What failure? You performed brilliantly!"

"We lost the village!"

"You were never meant to keep it!"

The goblin's eyes went wide as he stepped back and away from the fire.

"Then what was the *purpose*?"

"To show your might and let them all know that *you* are in command. And you performed the task admirably."

"You sent my men there to die just to show them I *could*?"

"No, *you* sent them there to die. *You* are their chief."

Gortogh fumed. His breath was fast and hard, and he worked to control himself.

"What do you care?" the elf said.

"They are my men!"

"Two weeks ago you were weak and powerless, and they would have run you through just for looking at them. Why care now?"

"Because I am their chief and the champion of Ogrosh. They are my people to protect."

He looked out to the goblins who were gathering and bowing on the ground outside the cave.

"I will find this girl and her dragon and gut them

both!" Gortogh said.

"A dragon?" the wizard said. "What kind of dragon?"

"I don't know! A woman and a dragon."

"A dragonmage?"

"I don't know! But I will find her and her dragon and make them pay."

"Let me deal with the dragonmage," Velanon said.

"They are my people to protect."

"They are yours to command, and they will die by your orders."

"How am I to help you with a third of my warriors dead? What good can I do now?"

"More will come," Velanon said. "You will have more warriors than you could possibly dream to command soon enough. This is only the beginning of what I have planned for you and your men."

"I do not like being a puppet, wizard."

"You are free to rule as you wish. They are your people. But know that I have my own designs here. You are a pawn I plucked from the mud to help me see them done. When you tire of taking my orders, do please tell me so that I can kill you and replace you with someone more loyal."

Gortogh was strong and powerful with the gifts Velanon had given him, but he knew the elf was right. Everything he had was because of the wizard. And he had no doubt that Velanon could take it all back at his whim and leave Gortogh nothing but a corpse.

He hung his head and sighed.

"What would you have me do?"

"Nothing," Velanon said. "You have done what I asked, and that is all that I ask for now. More tribes will come. In time you will become the champion of all the goblin tribes. I will come for you then. Take care of your people and do not meddle in the world of men any further. I wish for you and your army to remain hidden from their eyes for now."

The wizard stood and walked past him into the back of the cave.

"I will find and take care of this dragonmage soon enough," Velanon said. "For now, I have other business to attend to."

"When will we meet again?"

"When I am ready for you."

"What do I do until then?"

There was no answer from the darkness.

Gortogh sat on a log near the fire pit and rested his elbows on his knees. Closing his eyes, he breathed in the heat. He sat there for several minutes, enjoying the quiet, when he heard footsteps outside and someone call out.

"Mighty one?" someone called.

"What?" Gortogh said.

"Uh… more tribes come," the goblin said. "They come to see Ogrosh champion. They chiefs challenge you."

Gortogh sat stared into the fire. More will come.

"Chief?" the goblin said.

Gortogh closed his eyes for a moment before he stood and drew his longsword. He tightened his grip on the hilt and felt the power course through his muscles. He felt invincible. As though he were truly the champion of Ogrosh. With a last deep breath, Gortogh stepped into the sunlight with his arms and sword raised high.

"All will feel the might of Gortogh!"

Note from the Author

When I was 12 years old, my teacher gave us a reading assignment. A book that she had loved as a girl and had chosen for her class though none of the other classes chose such a book. It was barely considered literature, and even a little silly by most.

The book was J.R.R Tolkien's "The Hobbit". And within its pages, I found a love of books I had never known before. As a child, I never pretended to be a fireman or an army man. I always wanted to be a wizard. I did battle with mighty dragons and hordes of goblins. I imagined worlds of magic and sorcery. But I had never read a book about them. No one ever told me they were even out there.

I went on to ride dragons over Pern. I wandered across Prydain with Taran. I sailed the waves to Roke island with Sparrowhawk. And, of course, I followed Sam and Frodo into Mordor. I found in those books a lifelong love of fantasy.

All that time, I thought up my own stories. Not stories I wrote down, just stories I kept in my head. Some lived and died inside of me. Others came out for friends and their heroes to live and breathe around my Nana's kitchen table. But I never thought I would actually write a book that others would read. That was always just a secret dream.

As a lover of books, I know how precious a reader's time is. I thank you for giving me some of yours. I hope it was worth it for you.

Damon J Courtney
damon@damonjcourtney.com
January 11th, 2012

Now, a preview of what's to come…

The Burden of Faith
Dragon Bond Book 2

Prelude

The ogre chieftain's greatsword looked six feet long as it swung down to cleave Gortogh's head in two. Though, it was hard to tell from his current position on the ground. Things always appear larger looking up. Probably why the ogre looked ten feet tall himself.

Gortogh spread his legs and leaned back. The blade passed right before his eyes to slam into the ground. Even one as strong as the ogre chief moved slowly wielding a blade of that size, it seemed. Goblins were much quicker than their ogre cousins.

And Gortogh was quicker than most goblins.

As the ogre drew back to strike again, Gortogh flipped his legs over to roll back and to his knees. Pushing up, he bounced to his feet. It should have been an impressive display of balance and grace, but he had to stumble back another step to avoid losing his head. The greatsword passed just in front of his face for the second time. He steadied his feet and sized up his opponent.

He's bigger than ten feet.

The biggest Gortogh had ever seen. The ogre grinned a big, yellow-toothed grin as Gortogh tried to get his balance. He's just toying with me. Backing up another step, Gortogh felt a shove as one of the goblins ringing

219

them in a circle pushed him back in. He readied himself for another swing, but the ogre wasn't even paying attention. He was too busy walking around the circle with his arms wide and his sword held high.

The crowd of goblins booed and snarled while a small group of ogres on one side of the circle cheered and laughed. The ogre chieftain bathed in it all, the cheers and the jeers, and roared all the louder. This ogre would no doubt kill him in a fair fight. And so far, this had been a fair fight.

No more.

Gortogh squeezed the hilt of his sword and felt the magical power of the blade flow through him. His arms bulged, and he felt a sharp pain as his muscles grew and tightened against his stretched skin. In spite of himself, a little smile crept onto his lips as the ogre turned back to face him. Gortogh hated the fighting, but he found that he actually liked the idea of putting this ogre in his place.

Gortogh walked slowly and confidently across the circle, sword at the ready. The ogre obliged and came to meet him. They swung, their swords clanging loudly as they met. Unlike before, Gortogh's sword held strong, unyielding. The ogre's eyebrows flew up, but Gortogh revealed no emotion. As if nothing had changed. Their swords pushed against each other. The ogre's greatsword pushed against his magical blade, and Gortogh couldn't hide a little smile. With a shove of his other hand, he sent the ogre sprawling backward, arms flailing for balance. The brute managed to keep from falling as he stumbled back, but his attitude had vanished. Gortogh pointed his sword.

"Swear loyalty to Ogrosh champion!" Gortogh yelled. "Join us now. No more fighting."

The goblins cheered at the mention of their god and began chanting his name.

"Ogrosh! Ogrosh! Ogrosh!"

The ogres did not join the celebration. The chieftain's eyes narrowed. His massive hand tightened around the hilt of his greatsword. Gortogh saw the fury in his eyes and shook his head slowly from side to side.

Why must it always be this way?

"No make me kill you, Malakar," Gortogh said.

Gortogh truly did not want to kill the mighty ogre. He had killed far too many of Ogrosh's children in the last six months. Good warriors, all. Many of them the chiefs and champions of their own tribes. Some of the best goblin warriors he'd ever seen. They had all come to challenge him, to be Ogrosh's Champion.

And they had all died.

Such is the way of the children of Ogrosh.

Gortogh had offered each one a chance to swear loyalty, knowing that none would take it. Loyalty is earned through blood. When he killed Malakar, and he had no doubt that he would, the ogres of his tribe would swear their loyalty to him. Never had an ogre knelt before a goblin that Gortogh knew. They had always seen themselves above *puny* goblins.

But these ogres would kneel before him.

Malakar yelled and charged. Gortogh stood, unmoving, unblinking. The ogre swung his greatsword for his head. Still, Gortogh didn't move. Calmly raising his arm, the greatsword clanged off of his blade in a crash of metal. Gortogh's sword hummed and vibrated, his fingers going numb around the hilt, but the mighty swing had not even moved his hand.

Malakar rained blows down in rapid bursts, trying to drive Gortogh to his knees. Gortogh didn't move an inch. He was done dancing and dodging. Instead, he brought his sword to meet every blow, turning the greatsword aside with the flat of his blade. The sharp sound of metal on metal rang out through the trees and echoed off the mountains so loudly that some of the goblins covered their ears. But Gortogh did not flinch. He made no move to attack, only stood there and let the ogre see how easily he could turn aside every strike.

A cheer rolled through the goblin ranks.

It was a familiar sight for them. Gortogh heard their cheers, and it should have bolstered him, but it only deepened his sadness. Always more blood. The ogre stopped swinging, and Gortogh could see his chest heaving with each breath. Malakar was growing tired from his assault and could not keep it up. He stepped back and eyed the little goblin with renewed anger, and some suspicion.

"Me no want kill you, Malakar," Gortogh said calmly.

The ogre charged again and tried to shove him back from his stance. Gortogh set his foot and met the charge head on. The brute smashed into him with a force Gortogh had not felt in all his fights with other goblins.

The ogre was more than twice his size, and he had clearly underestimated his strength. Gortogh flew through the air and landed near the edge of the circle with a great crash, barely keeping hold of his sword.

A cheer went up from the ogres this time, and Malakar held his arms wide and turned in a circle. He roared at the prone goblin and laughed.

"You are not champion of Ogrosh! You are weak and puny goblin! Champion of Ogrosh should be him chosen people! Ogres bear name of Ogrosh!"

The ogres cheered again, louder this time. Gortogh was still trying to recover from the jarring hit. His head was muddled, and he felt a sharp pain in his chest that made it hard to breathe. With the strength of magic flowing through his veins, he managed to put his hands down and push to a kneeling position.

"Yes! Kneel before mighty Malakar!"

Gortogh grimaced and felt for the hilt of his sword. His hand closed around it, and he waited, his breaths shallow and stinging. Time to end this.

Malakar did a few more turns for the crowd and then charged with a great yell. His sword was high, ready to deliver a killing blow. Gortogh remained on his knees until the ogre was almost to him. Tensing every muscle in his body, Gortogh leapt to his feet. As the greatsword swung down for his head, he stepped under it and raised his own blade. The magical longsword hummed with power, almost hungry.

It sliced cleanly through the brute's arm just above the elbow.

The arm went tumbling through the air with the greatsword still in its grip and landed at the feet of the crowd who stumbled back in stunned silence. Malakar looked at his arm lying on the ground. Confusion flooded his face. Then his eyes went to the other half of it that still hung from his shoulder, spurting blood.

The ogre bellowed and screamed and stumbled around the circle in pain. Gortogh stood calmly, waiting for rage to replace the panic and pain. It always does. Malakar howled some more and staggered a few more steps before falling to his knees and holding the stump of his arm. A growl formed deep in his chest. His head shot up and his eyes burned into Gortogh, his whole body trembling.

There's the rage.

With a roar, he stood as one of the ogres behind him helped him to his feet and tied a leather cord around the remainder of his arm. Blood poured from the stump, but Malakar didn't seem to care. With his remaining hand, he grabbed the other ogre's sword and charged. Gortogh went forward to meet him. As their swords clashed again, he could feel the depleted strength behind the blows. The loss of blood and his sword arm left Malakar with very little ability to continue this fight. But he would continue, Gortogh knew.

He will fight with every last breath.

Gortogh dodged under a wild swing and kicked out with his foot, catching the ogre in the gut. Malakar stumbled back, his sword tip dipping into the dirt. He no longer had the strength to keep it up. He tried to steady himself, but Gortogh kicked him again, knocking him to the ground.

Ten feet of ogre hitting the ground makes an awfully big thud. The circle shook, and the gathered goblins cheered and jeered. The ogre tribe tightened ranks and drew their swords. The goblins all cheered and cried out in unison.

"Fry! Fry! Fry! Fry!"

This is what they came to see.

It's what they always want.

They wanted Gortogh to release the lightning magic stored in his wicked sword and destroy the ogre chieftain. Gortogh wanted this to end *now*. No more blood. No more magic. He hated using magic to best his opponents. Except for the magic he used to make himself stronger and more agile, of course. Without that, the fight would have been over in seconds and with a *very* different outcome.

The first chiefs of the goblin tribes that joined him all had fought him in that same ring. They had come seeking glory at besting the champion of Ogrosh. In those battles, Gortogh would fight with *all* of his might and magic. He stoked the crowd with laughs and hand waving just as Malakar had done. He enjoyed it. Reveled in it. When his opponents were all but dead, he would offer them one last chance to join him. When they refused, and they all refused, he would unleash the lightning in his sword and fry them.

"Fry! Fry! Fry! Fry!"

They wanted Malakar to fry.

The bloodthirsty goblins always wanted to see the most spectacular end. Gortogh had lost his taste for it. Too many strong warriors had died at his hand. For no reason other than to show his superiority. He wished, just once, they would join him without a fight.

But that was not the way of the children of Ogrosh.

The ogre chief pushed himself to stand and faced Gortogh with a grimace. He had one good arm and a strong sword. In a fight with any ordinary goblin, that would have been more than enough. But Gortogh was no ordinary goblin. If what the goblins believed was true, he was imbued with the power of his god. If Malakar had believed it, he might have accepted the offer to join without a fight.

If only he'd believed the lie.

Both combatants stood steadfast and waited for the other. The goblins surrounding the circle continued their chant. The ogres on the far end had formed a tight cluster around themselves with their weapons drawn. Gortogh looked around the crowd and then back to the ogre chieftain. They stared long and hard at each other as the chants grew louder and more insistent. Paying no attention to them, Gortogh lowered his sword and motioned Malakar over with a wave of his hand.

Malakar's brow creased. He brought his sword up with his remaining hand, the blood dripping steadily from the stump of his other arm. Gortogh made no move toward him but simply waved his hand again. When the brute refused to move, Gortogh reached his hand back and slid his sword into the leather scabbard that hung from a belt over his shoulder. The ogre's brow scrunched up even more, and Gortogh waved again.

The crowd grew silent.

The cheering stopped, and the goblins stared in confusion. This was not how the fight was supposed to go. Malakar took a few cautious steps toward him, and Gortogh waved once more, never inching toward his weapon. The big ogre let his sword slip to his side as he took a few more steps toward the center of the ring.

He looked back at the ogre tribe, but they all just watched in silence. A few more steps brought him within striking distance, but Gortogh made no move for his sword. He waited patiently for the ogre to draw nearer. Once he was close enough, Gortogh leaned forward and spoke.

"Join us. I will not make you kneel. You can lead your ogres as your own tribe under my command."

The ogre's eyes narrowed.

"I don't want to kill you," Gortogh said.

Malakar continued to stare but said nothing. Gortogh could see the thoughts playing out on his face. He had to know that he would lose this fight and most likely his life. He was being offered a chance to live, but it went against the ways of the tribes.

"We *all* fight for Ogrosh," Gortogh said. "You will still be chief of the ogres. You will lead the tribes as my commander."

Malakar straightened and looked around at the goblins watching silently with great interest. He looked at the ogres of his tribe, but they looked just as confused as the goblins. He looked back at Gortogh and stared long and hard. Seconds passed in total silence with the whole crowd watching. Slowly, the ogre nodded his head as the tip of his sword dipped to the ground. He turned to address the circle.

"We will join champion of Ogrosh!" he shouted. "I will lead ogre tribe in Ogrosh name!"

Gortogh breathed a little sigh of relief and watched as confusion registered on all the goblins gathered. No one cheered as he had hoped. It was the opposite, in fact. Once the realization dawned that there would be no spectacular bloodletting, many began to boo and growl. More howls quickly joined them. Weapons were drawn.

They called out for blood.

They called out for him to fry.

Gortogh snatched his sword out in a quick motion. Malakar jumped and brought his own blade back up, but Gortogh was already turning away. With a single thought, the energy stored in his sword coursed down the blade and then leapt from the tip in an arc of blue lightning.

It shot through the air with a loud thunderclap and struck a tree high above the crowd. The trunk of the tree splintered and cracked in a great explosion, sending shards of wood flying. Gortogh held the sword high and turned in a circle to meet their eyes, challenging any to disagree.

"I am the will of Ogrosh!" he shouted.

The goblins fell silent. No one dared speak or jeer. Gortogh turned back to Malakar who was staring in amazement at the blackened tree that was now missing a huge chunk on one side. The ogre looked down at him with his eyes wide, staring, unmoving. His face cracked into a toothy smile. Then the smile turned to laughter.

"Boom!" he shouted and laughed louder.

The goblins began laughing with him, and Gortogh sighed with relief.

"We fight for Ogrosh!" Malakar shouted. "For Ogrosh! For Ogrosh!"

The crowd took up his chant and shouted to the heavens. Malakar stood beside Gortogh and shouted for Ogrosh. Even Gortogh got caught up in the fervor and shouted to the blood god. He watched the ogres who were still looking on with confusion, but they began to chant as well.

For Ogrosh.

All for Ogrosh.

With a slap on Gortogh's back, Malakar went to stand with his ogres, still chanting. Gortogh turned and walked to the other side where the goblins were cheering and chanting as one.

"For Ogrosh! For Ogrosh!"

Over his shoulder, Gortogh heard a great yell, followed by the unmistakable sound of a sword cleaving through flesh and bone. He spun back in time to see Malakar's head roll from his shoulders and fall unceremoniously to the dirt. It rolled several turns before coming to rest in the middle of the ring. His mouth still turned up in a smile as the lifeless eyes stared at Gortogh.

The headless body tumble backward with a thud that shook the circle. The cheering stopped in the moment it took them all to realize something had happened. Goblins in the back were pushing and scrambling forward to try and see what was going on.

Gortogh stared into the eyes of the ogre holding a bloody greatsword in his hand. Malakar's greatsword. Matching his stare, without looking away, he raised the sword high above his head. Blood dripped from the blade to land on his shoulders and head, but he held Gortogh's gaze and paid it no attention.

"I am Brog!" he yelled. "*I* am ogre chieftain!"

Everyone stood in stunned silence. Some of the ogres behind Brog looked confused. Many more were smiling or nodding. Some even laughed. Brog's gaze drifted around the circle, meeting the eyes of the goblins.

"We fight for Ogrosh!" he shouted.

Without missing a beat, the goblins took up their chant again, louder this time. Gortogh met Brog's stare as his eyes came back around. Gortogh turned and strode from the circle without another word. The crowd parted at his approach, some falling to kneel before him. A great cheer went up from the goblins as some jumped into the circle to tear the body apart and play sport with the severed head.

Such is the way of the children of Ogrosh.